As Elizabeth rode the wave, she couldn't help but feel that something was wrong. Usually at this point in a ride, she felt in control. But right then she felt just the opposite.

She glanced over her shoulder and saw the huge wave beginning to crash down on top of her. She tried to brace herself for the impact, and then she took a deep breath.

The water crashed over her, and the surfboard slipped out from under her. Just as Elizabeth was rising to the surface to get another breath, she felt a powerful thud on the side of her head, and then suddenly everything went blurry.

Elizabeth was sinking deeper into the wave when she felt a strong current catch hold of her. It dragged her down as if a great chain were attached to her legs, pulling her deeper and deeper into the water.

Elizabeth suddenly felt her heart constrict. *I'm caught in a riptide*, she suddenly realized.

Her body was crying out for air. Forgetting for a moment that she was underwater, she took a desperate breath. Then everything went black as n

D1017730

SWEET VALLEY HIGH

THE NEW ELIZABETH

Written by
Kate William

Created by
FRANCINE PASCAL

BANTAM BOOKS
NEW YORK · TORONTO · LONDON · SYDNEY · AUCKLAND

RL 6, IL age 12 and up

THE NEW ELIZABETH
A Bantam Book / March 1990

Sweet Valley High is a registered trademark of Francine Pascal

Conceived by Francine Pascal

Produced by David Weiss Associates, Inc.
33 West 17th Street
New York, NY 10011

Cover art by James Mathewuse

ISBN 0-553-28385-5

Published simultaneously in the United States and Canada

Bantam Books are published by Bantam Books, a division of Bantam Doubleday Dell Publishing Group, Inc. Its trademark, consisting of the words "Bantam Books" and the portrayal of a rooster, is Registered in U.S. Patent and Trademark Office and in other countries. Marca Registrada. Bantam Books, 666 Fifth Avenue, New York, New York 10103.

PRINTED IN THE UNITED STATES OF AMERICA

OPM   0 9 8 7 6 5 4 3 2 1

THE NEW
ELIZABETH

One

"Watch out, everyone! Here comes Elizabeth Wakefield, the trend-setting fashion queen of Sweet Valley High, with her daring new perm," Lila Fowler announced.

Jessica Wakefield, Lila Fowler, and Amy Sutton were having lunch together in the cafeteria, and things had been fairly boring until Lila spotted Elizabeth—with her curly, shoulder-length blond perm—making her way through the crowd. And then the teasing began.

"Yeah, Liz's perm sure is wild and crazy," Amy responded.

"Let's just say your sister has a weird way of being adventurous, Jess," Lila continued, munching on a potato chip. "I mean, some people drive race cars, climb mountains, or sail boats around the world, but Elizabeth gets her hair curled."

Jessica laughed and glanced across the crowded cafeteria at her twin. She had been as surprised

1

as anyone when Elizabeth showed up a week earlier with a perm. She knew it was all part of Elizabeth's new plan to be spontaneous and to take risks, but unless Elizabeth did something a little more daring, Jessica was not going to be impressed.

"Just remember, Lila," Jessica said, holding her chin high, "not everybody can be as *daring* and *spontaneous* as I am."

"Thank goodness for that," Amy said. "I mean, could you imagine a world full of Jessica Wakefields? It would be utter chaos."

"But imagine a world full of *Elizabeth* Wakefields," Lila said. "Could you imagine a duller, more predictable place? I think I'd go crazy."

"Hey, Jess," Elizabeth said, sliding into the empty chair beside her twin. "Can I use the car this afternoon? I want to check out the History of Communication exhibit at the museum. It's supposed to be really good."

"Now, that's the boring Elizabeth Wakefield we're used to," Lila whispered to Amy.

"Are you guys laughing at my perm again?" Elizabeth asked, annoyed.

"Oh, no, Liz. We all like your hair," Jessica answered, sending a glance to her friends.

"We think it's really cute." Amy smiled at Elizabeth. "But lots of people get perms. It's not really the most daring thing in the world."

"Face it, Liz," Lila added. "Jess is the risk-taker in your family. She loves the smell of danger. You're happy just to write for *The Oracle* and go to the museum.''

"This exhibit happens to be one of the best in the country,'' Elizabeth said.

"Oh, I'm sure it is!'' Lila laughed. "We'll see you later,'' she said, and she and Amy stood up and walked off to another table.

Elizabeth sat perfectly still for a moment, stung by Lila's words. Lila was not exactly Elizabeth's favorite person, even though she was Jessica's best friend. Lila could be a little mean, and very snobbish, but this time, Elizabeth had to admit that Lila had a point.

"Don't let those two worry you, Liz,'' Jessica began, glancing at her twin and taking a big bite out of her sandwich. "Just because I'm the one who takes all the risks and does all the interesting things doesn't mean you aren't a good person or anything.''

"Gee, thanks,'' Elizabeth said.

Physically the beautiful twins were identical in almost every way, from their sparkling blue-green eyes to their perfect, willowy size-six figures. But as far as their personalities, the twins were definitely *not* identical. Elizabeth was born four minutes before Jessica, and she always joked that those extra minutes made her more responsible, thoughtful, and mature. Elizabeth was serious about her schoolwork, and although she

3

liked a good party, she was just as happy to spend a quiet evening with her boyfriend, Todd Wilkins, or with her best friend, Enid Rollins. She spent a lot of time writing for *The Oracle*, Sweet Valley High's student newspaper, and she hoped someday to be a professional writer. Elizabeth loved sports and music and dancing, but she could also get excited about going to a museum.

Jessica was impulsive and always lived for the moment. When it came to boyfriends, for instance, Jessica didn't like to be tied down. Except for a brief relationship recently with A. J. Morgan, Jessica had never stayed with one boy for long. There were always too many other cute ones around!

Of the twins, there was no doubt in anyone's mind that Jessica was the risk-taker. But Elizabeth was beginning to get tired of her conservative, sensible reputation. And now she was wondering how to change things, once and for all.

I've got to prove that I can live dangerously, too. Elizabeth ran her hand distractedly through her hair. *But how?*

Just then an idea dawned on her, and her eyes sparkled.

I do need the car this afternoon, she thought with a determined smile. *But I won't be visiting the museum!*

Elizabeth waited until she heard her sister talking to Lila on the phone. Then she collected all her magazines and hurried out to the car.

Jessica will sure be in for a big surprise, she thought as she revved up the engine. *And so will everyone else!*

Ten minutes later Elizabeth pulled the red Fiat she shared with Jessica into a parking space in downtown Sweet Valley. She marched into the sporting goods store and started looking around. All of the equipment was incredible! First she looked at a beautiful pair of clear blue plastic flippers, leaning up against a scuba tank. Right beside those she saw a deep-sea mask made of matching blue plastic and a hot-pink wet suit.

She could see it now: she would be a scuba diver and find sunken treasures. She would discover the skeletons of Spanish galleons lost at sea and then appear on the cover of *National Geographic*—in the hot-pink wet suit—her hands full of gold coins.

But then a multicolored hang glider in the corner of the store caught her eye. She took a deep breath and imagined how it would feel to run off of a cliff, supported by fragile wings. She would look so small to all her friends, who would be watching her in amazement from the ground below. That would show them who could take a *real* risk!

She hurried over to the salesperson. "Excuse me. I'm interested in buying some scuba gear, or maybe a hang glider," Elizabeth said boldly. The salesman looked up from the inventory list he was reviewing. He seemed a little surprised, but he dutifully followed Elizabeth over to the scuba gear.

"Now, I definitely want the hot-pink wet suit," Elizabeth began quickly, trying to sound as if she had been deep-sea diving for years. "And these blue flippers and the matching mask. And then one of these oxygen tanks."

"Fine," the salesman slowly replied. "You'll also need to get an air compressor and a mouthpiece. I assume you've never done any scuba diving before?"

"Uh, no, I haven't," Elizabeth admitted. "But I'm ready to go for it."

"Then you'll need lessons to get your certification," he said. "And that may take a couple of months."

"A couple of months?" Elizabeth repeated. But she wanted to start her new adventurous life *now*.

"How much does all of this equipment cost?" she asked the salesman.

"The suit is three hundred dollars," he said. "And this air compressor costs two hundred and fifty. The masks and flippers are the best on the market, imported from France, and they're on sale this week for a hundred and fifty." *One hundred and fifty dollars for a lousy pair of flippers?* Elizabeth thought, aghast. *I can't afford all this!*

"But you can take lessons and rent the equipment first, to see if you like it," the salesman suggested.

"Oh, how much are lessons?" Elizabeth asked.

"Fifty dollars an hour," he said.

Elizabeth's heart dropped. "Maybe I'd better try hang gliding instead."

"That's pretty expensive, too," the salesman said gently, sensing that Elizabeth was discouraged by the prices.

Elizabeth nodded glumly. "Well, how much is that pretty, multicolored one in the corner?"

"Oh, that's a fancy new one," the salesman answered. "But I can sell you a nice used hang glider for about seven hundred dollars."

Elizabeth shook her head. She was beginning to think that being adventurous was completely impractical—and expensive. No wonder Jessica always ended up getting in over her head! Elizabeth couldn't ask her parents for any money because she wanted her new hobby to be a surprise. And she certainly didn't have seven hundred dollars of her own to throw around.

"Thanks for your help," Elizabeth told the salesman.

"You're welcome," he said cheerfully.

On her way out of the store, Elizabeth noticed a small sign in the window:

"Surfing Lessons. Only Seven Dollars an Hour. Moon Beach Surf Club, Big Mesa. Rental Boards Available."

A wide smile crossed Elizabeth's face. Of course—surfing! No one would ever expect to see *her* riding those huge waves. And even she could afford seven dollars an hour!

Half an hour later Elizabeth pulled into a parking lot behind a small weather-beaten clubhouse. Moon Beach was long and wide, and the sand was white. Elizabeth could see a few surfers out in the water, and for a moment she watched them glide along the curling waves. Her heart began to beat faster. The surfers moved so gracefully, and it didn't look too difficult, either. Why hadn't she thought of this earlier?

Just then, one of the surfers she had been watching flew up into the air, his board soaring high above him. He crashed into the water and began swimming frantically after his board.

I guess it's not as easy as it looks, Elizabeth thought, her heart sinking a little. *But I didn't want to do something safe and easy, did I?*

The sign above the clubhouse door read: Moon Beach Surf Club. This beach would be perfect for her—especially since kids from Sweet Valley rarely came this far north. Elizabeth could learn surfing in complete secrecy, just as she had planned.

As she stepped out of her car, Elizabeth heard the sound of laughter coming from the clubhouse. She glanced through the window and saw three boys and a pretty girl having a lively conversation. One boy, with lime-green zinc oxide on his nose, was wildly waving his arms to make a point. He was tall and darkly tanned, with longish, sun-streaked blond hair and a lean and muscular body. Elizabeth smiled at his wild gestures and opened the door.

"And *she's* the one!" The boy with the zinc oxide on his nose pointed at Elizabeth and smiled. "Congratulations," he continued. "You win the prize!"

Elizabeth looked puzzled. "Um, I saw an ad in a sports store in Sweet Valley for surfing les—"

"That's great!" the boy interrupted her. "But you've just won the lottery—the surfing lottery! Hi, my name is Sean Blake."

"I'm Elizabeth Wakefield—Liz," she replied, shaking Sean's hand.

The two boys behind the counter introduced themselves as Sammy and Dave. They said they all worked at the clubhouse after school and on weekends, renting boards and selling equipment and sodas. Sean was a senior at Big Mesa High, and the other boys were juniors, like Elizabeth.

"I'm Laurie MacNeil," the girl said. "It's nice to meet you."

"You, too," Elizabeth said. "Do you go to Big Mesa?"

Laurie nodded. "I'm a senior, like Sean."

"Liz, have you ever surfed before?" Sean asked. His gold-flecked green eyes sparkled.

"No," Elizabeth replied. "And I've never done anything *like* it, either. But I really want to try something new—you know, to surprise my friends."

"All right!" Sean exclaimed. "That's perfect."

"Huh?" Elizabeth asked, confused.

"Don't worry about a thing. I plan to make you into a *great* surfer," Sean replied. "All you have to do is agree to take lessons from me."

Elizabeth hesitated for a moment, trying to make up her mind. Was surfing what she really wanted to do?

"They're free!" Sean added.

"Free?" Elizabeth repeated.

"Sure. I'll even throw in the rental board," Sean said. "And I guarantee that your friends will be impressed."

"You've got a deal!" Elizabeth exclaimed.

Two

Before she knew what was happening, Elizabeth had agreed to a month of surfing lessons. Now Sean was busy showing her the club's collection of rental boards.

"This one's a classic Malibu, all foam with a fiberglass top," he began. "The skeg's a little wacky so you get some chatter, but it's not a bad semi-gun board if you ride it close to the crest. But come to think of it, Liz, for you maybe—"

"Wait a minute!" Elizabeth cried, holding up her hand. "I can't understand a word you're saying."

"What's wrong, am I talking too fast?" Sean replaced the surfboard he was holding and looked at Elizabeth.

"Too fast?" Elizabeth repeated. "Not only are you talking too fast, but you're using a foreign language."

At that, the boys behind the counter laughed.

"You've just met Mr. Surfing Encyclopedia," Sammy joked as he polished a new board.

"You'll probably wish you'd never heard of surfing when he's done with you," Dave responded, smiling.

"Sean may be a great *surfer*, but we'll have to wait and see what kind of *teacher* he is," Sammy added. "I get the feeling we may be seeing Sean around here for a few weekend shifts. Don't you, Laurie?"

Laurie smiled. "Definitely."

"What are you guys talking about?" Elizabeth asked. She was beginning to be sorry she had ever seen the notice for surfing lessons.

"I'm sorry, Liz," Sean began, flashing her a big smile. "I guess we do owe you a little explanation."

Elizabeth sank down into an old upholstered chair. "That would help."

Sean perched on the arm of her chair. "Just before you came in, we were trying to decide whether it takes a lot of raw talent to be a great surfer or just a little bit of determination . . . and a great teacher." Sean puffed out his chest and raised one eyebrow. A crumpled ball of paper flew across the counter and hit his arm.

"And guess who considers himself a *great* teacher?" Sammy joked.

"So, I made a little bet with everyone here," Sean continued, hurling the paper back at

14

Sammy. "I said I'd take the next person who happened to walk through the door as my student. And I bet that after only a month of lessons with *me*, that person would place in the Moon Beach Surfing Competition at the end of the month. If I win, and that means if *you* win, Liz, then Sammy and Dave have to chip in and buy me a new board. If I lose, then I have to work the weekend shift for the next three months. And you happened to be the next person to walk through the door!"

Elizabeth could hardly believe her good luck. A big public competition would be the perfect opportunity to show everyone what she had been up to—and that she could do more than museum-hop.

"We'll need a lot of practice for the competition, so we'll meet here three afternoons a week for hour-long lessons," Sean continued, crossing his muscular arms. "How does next Tuesday sound for the first lesson?"

Elizabeth tried to hide a knowing smile. She didn't think she had ever met such a cocky, confident guy in all her life. Sean just *assumed* she would go along with whatever he offered. But she had to admit, everything he said fit in perfectly with her plans.

"That'll be fine, Sean," Elizabeth answered, standing up to leave. She knew that three days a week was a lot of time. She was usually pretty busy after school, either writing for *The Oracle* or spending time with Todd. But she was determined to become a surfer in time for the championship.

"Then it's all settled!" Sean exclaimed, jumping to his feet. He grabbed Elizabeth's hand and gave it a hearty shake. "Watch out, you guys. Elizabeth Wakefield is about to become one of California's hottest surfers!"

Laurie MacNeil leaned her head back against the wall and watched Elizabeth leave the clubhouse. She hated to admit it, but her heart had sunk as soon as Elizabeth walked through the door. Why couldn't a boy have come in, or at least a girl who wasn't *quite* as pretty and outgoing as Elizabeth Wakefield?

Liz is just Sean's type. And now he'll be spending lots of time with her because of the bet, she thought.

Laurie quickly checked her watch and saw it was time for her to get back to work. She had a job at the Moon Beach Ice Cream Parlor, which was a few doors down from the surf club. Usually she liked the thought of serving ice cream and seeing all her friends, but right now she felt more like being alone.

"My break is over, guys," she said, rising slowly from her chair. "I'll see you later."

Sean was busy talking to Sammy and Dave

about the big bet and hardly threw a glance in her direction.

Laurie shut the door behind her, then stopped on the sandy path to take a deep breath. *Everything is going to be just fine*, she told herself. *Sean and I have known each other for a long time, and we have something very special.*

She had known Sean since they were small, and she had always liked him. This year they had spent a lot of time hanging around together —especially since Laurie started working at the ice cream parlor. She didn't surf, but she spent almost all of her breaks in the clubhouse with Sean and his friends.

Laurie was just about to leave when she heard the boys' voices from inside the clubhouse. She hated eavesdropping, but she couldn't help over-hearing a sentence or two.

"Liz is really pretty," Dave said.

"You may be a winner even if you lose the bet," Sammy added.

"Maybe so," Sean replied, laughing.

Laurie turned and hurried away across the sand. She didn't want to hear any more about Elizabeth Wakefield. Right beside the clubhouse was a café where lots of Big Mesa students hung out after school and on weekends. As she passed the café Laurie couldn't help but think of the previous Saturday, when she and Sean had sat there together. Sean had asked her out to a movie, and that very night they had gone on their first real date. Nothing major had happened, but they had had a good time, and Laurie hoped it would be the start of something great.

But now, with Elizabeth in the picture, Laurie had the sinking feeling her romantic relationship with Sean had just ended.

She hurried past the café, hoping that none of her friends would notice her.

"Hey, Laurie," John Monroe called out. "What's going on in the clubhouse?"

"Strategic planning for the big competition next month, right?" Phil Carter added.

"You could say that," Laurie admitted with a shy smile.

"Did they convince you to enter it yet?" Phil asked.

Laurie shook her head. "No way! You know I don't surf."

"But you must know all the moves, since you hang out with Supersurfman himself," John said with a smile.

"Not really." Laurie wrinkled her nose. "I mean, it's one thing to know what they do, but actually getting out there and doing it is another story. Anyway, I'm too busy working to be a surf bum. I'll see you guys later. Have a good weekend!"

"OK, Laur. Catch you Monday," Phil said.

Laurie walked into the ice cream parlor and slipped her apron on over her clothes. As she moved behind the counter, she couldn't help thinking that maybe John Monroe had been right. She *did* know a lot about surfing; she listened to the guys at the clubhouse talk about it nonstop. And she had to admit that she was a natural athlete. She never had had any trouble picking up a new sport.

Maybe I will learn to surf for the big competition, she thought. *I could show Sean that I'm more than just the girl next door.*

On Monday at lunch, Elizabeth sneaked up behind her boyfriend, gave him a quick kiss on the ear, and then sat down beside him.

"Who are you?" Todd asked, a glow coming to his coffee-colored eyes.

"Your long-lost girlfriend," Elizabeth answered brightly. "I thought I'd never get out of class."

"Well, I'm glad you did," Todd answered. "Speaking of which, I forgot to ask you how the exhibit was at the museum last Friday."

Elizabeth started unpacking her lunch bag. "Let's just say it was more exciting than I expected."

"Liz, you're about the only person I know who gets excited about museums," Todd responded.

"What's that supposed to mean?" Elizabeth asked. "That I'm dull and boring and completely predictable?"

"Of course not," Todd said, sipping his milk. "It just means that you're—different, that's all."

"I'm not sure how much I like the word *different*," Elizabeth said. "That's what my father says whenever Jessica cooks dinner. 'Well . . . it's different.' "

Todd laughed. "He's right—I've tasted her cooking. But you know I meant different in a good way—as in unique. I really *don't* know anyone like you." He reached over and squeezed Elizabeth's hands. "OK?"

"I guess so," she said, smiling.

"Good. So are you ready to hit the courts tomorrow? It'll be fun to play a few games together. We haven't done that in a while," Todd said.

Suddenly all the blood drained from Elizabeth's face. She had forgotten all about their tennis date. And tomorrow was Tuesday—the day of her very first surfing lesson. There was no way she could miss *that*.

"Did we have a tennis date for Tuesday, Todd?" Elizabeth asked sheepishly, stalling for time while she searched for a good excuse.

"Don't you remember, Liz?" Todd said. "I was going to help you with your serve."

"Oh, Todd, now I remember, but . . ." Elizabeth looked down at her tray and thought for a moment. She didn't like misleading Todd, but she wanted the big surfing competition at the end of the month to be a complete surprise.

"It sounds like you've made other plans," Todd finally said.

Elizabeth paused before saying, "Well, I'm doing this extra-credit project at Moon Beach. You know, out at the Marine Biology Center. And I'm supposed to be there Tuesday after school. We're just getting started, actually."

"Marine biology," Todd mused. "You mean like tide pools and turtle eggs and slimy seaweed?"

"Exactly," Elizabeth replied, laughing. "I guess I became interested in it after our field trip out to Anacapa Island."

"Uh-oh," Todd said. "You're not going to get shipwrecked like your sister did, are you?"

"No way."

"I guess I don't really need to worry about you, anyway," Todd said, leaning back in his chair. "Jessica is the one who's always getting into trouble, not you. Jessica and her crazy adventures." Todd chuckled and gently nodded his head. "A *marine biology* project! How much *safer* can you get?"

"Do you mean how much more *boring* can you get?" Elizabeth asked.

"Well . . ." Todd shrugged playfully.

"Liz!" Jessica's voice rang out suddenly from

across the crowded cafeteria. Elizabeth turned around and saw her twin hurrying toward her.

"Hi, Jessica," she said pleasantly.

"Liz, I'm completely humiliated!" Jessica moaned, nearly collapsing into the chair beside her sister.

"What are you talking about?" Elizabeth asked.

Jessica opened her mouth to speak, but before she had a chance to say a word, Winston Egbert sneaked up behind her and tapped her on the shoulder.

"Well, if it isn't Magenta Galaxy," Winston said, grinning. "Do you think I could borrow your Psychedelic Overtones tape?"

"Winston," Jessica growled, "you're treading on very thin ice!"

"Oh, pardon me," Winston continued in a snobby, sophisticated voice. "You're not Magenta Galaxy. You must be the famous, sophisticated Daniella Fromage! I was wondering if you could interpret that experimental theater piece we saw last week."

Magenta Galaxy and Daniella Fromage were the two names—for the two different personalities—that Jessica had invented to help her attract interesting guys from a computer dating service she had signed up with a couple of weeks earlier. The plan had backfired when she found out that the interesting guys she met had invented names and personalities every bit as phony as hers.

Elizabeth was having a hard time keeping herself from laughing out loud at Winston's performance.

"That's very funny, Winston," Jessica snapped. "But if you don't tell me *exactly* who told you that story in *exactly* two and a half seconds, I'm going to perform some experimental theater on your *face!*"

"Don't do that," Winston said, bringing his hands to his mouth. "I'll talk! I heard about your latest adventure from Caroline Pearce."

"Caroline Pearce!" Jessica exclaimed, crossing her arms. "I should have known she couldn't stop gossiping for long," Jessica said, fuming.

"I really thought she had quit," Elizabeth answered sadly. "Especially after all her gossiping blew up in her face."

"Don't get me wrong, Liz. I don't care if she spreads rumors," Jessica snapped. "But when she spreads them about *me* . . . then that means war!"

"But, Jessica, they're not rumors," Elizabeth reminded her twin. "The story *is* true."

"Wait a second, Elizabeth. Whose side are you on, anyway? I mean, even Aaron Dallas called me Magenta Galaxy in the hall today. Everybody knows about it!"

"Maybe Aaron likes this Magenta person," Todd suggested, grinning.

Elizabeth giggled. "Wait until he meets Daniella."

"Look, I know you two think this is very funny," Jessica said, standing up to leave. "But I can tell you something right now. Caroline Pearce won't be laughing when I'm through with her."

"What are you going to do, Jess?" Elizabeth asked.

"Get revenge!" Jessica shouted.

Three

On Tuesday afternoon Elizabeth pulled the Fiat to a stop in the parking lot of the Moon Beach Surf Club. While sitting in the car for a moment, Elizabeth took a deep breath and looked out at the ocean just beyond. *This is the moment to prove you can be as daring as anybody*, she thought. But her spirits sank when she got out of the car and saw the size of the crashing waves. She had always loved the ocean and was a strong swimmer, but she had never really ventured out too far from shore.

"Hi, Liz!" Sean Blake called to her from the clubhouse door. "Ready to go? Let's find you the perfect surfboard."

"Hi, Sean," Elizabeth said as she walked over to the little shack. The whole place smelled of wax and sea salt.

"Let's see," Sean said, stepping back and studying Elizabeth. "How tall are you?"

"Five feet six," Elizabeth told him.

"Hmmm." Sean sifted through the boards. "I want to give you one of our best boards. It'll move a lot faster in the water."

"I'd rather have a slow one, actually," Elizabeth said and laughed.

"Don't sell yourself short, Liz," Sean answered. He chose a purple board with a hot-pink stripe down the middle and headed out on to the beach. "It may take a lot of work—and maybe even a little bit of overtime," he added with a significant glance at Elizabeth. "But I'll make you into a surfer. I promise."

Sean sure is confident, Elizabeth thought, *and a little bit too friendly sometimes*. As they walked down to the water, Elizabeth saw a surfer wipe out in the waves offshore. His board flew up above him, and he went sprawling into the waves. Suddenly Elizabeth's stomach started to churn.

"Did you see that wipeout?" Sean asked, pointing at the ocean. He swept his blond hair back and stopped in the middle of the beach. "Let that be a warning to you that there's more to surfing than riding the curl. Safety always comes first, OK?"

"OK." Elizabeth smiled. She slipped off her sandals and began to take off her shorts.

"Are you a good swimmer?" Sean asked.

"We have a pool in our backyard," Elizabeth replied. "I practically grew up in the water."

26

"Good. Now, the first thing you should know is you *always* use the ankle strap." He showed her how to attach the strap to her ankle. "That way you'll never lose your board. But that doesn't mean your board can't pearl, and if—"

"Pearl?" Elizabeth interrupted. "What does that mean?"

"When your board shoots up from under you and goes flying into the air, that's called pearling—like what happened to the guy who just wiped out. And pearling is one of the most dangerous things about surfing. The board can come down on top of you and give you a pretty good whack in the head. That's how most surfing fatalities happen."

Elizabeth swallowed hard as she pulled off her T-shirt. This kind of talk sure wasn't helping her nervousness!

"To prevent pearling, just make sure the nose of the board doesn't dip under the water," Sean continued, kneeling down in the sand and removing a stick of wax from a small bag. "But before we talk about anything else, let's wax this board of yours."

Sean started to rub the wax across the purple board. "What's the wax for?" Elizabeth asked.

"Without wax," Sean answered, "fiberglass can be pretty slippery. Some boards need more wax than others, and you can tell by . . ." As Sean lectured and rubbed the wax into the board,

27

Elizabeth removed a bottle of suntan oil and was about to spread it on her shoulders.

"And you should always wax in the sun, so the wax melts faster." Suddenly Sean looked up at Elizabeth. "Stop! Stop right there!" he cried.

"What's wrong?" Elizabeth asked.

"You should never use tanning oil when you're surfing," he continued. "If you do, I guarantee your board will be as slick as a greased frying pan. You won't be able to stand up for a second."

"But I don't want to burn in the sun," Elizabeth said.

Sean removed a plastic tube from his bag. "Here's some special tanning cream. It's not greasy and won't make you slip and wipe out. Want me to spread some on your back?"

"No, thanks," Elizabeth said. "I can do it."

"Are you sure?" Sean asked, lifting his eyebrows suggestively. "I wouldn't mind."

"I think I can handle it myself," Elizabeth said. *What a flirt!* she thought.

Sean handed her the tanning cream. As he talked about beginning surfing techniques, Elizabeth listened intently and smoothed the cream over her shoulders and arms.

"So the next thing you do after attaching your ankle strap is kneel on your board and paddle out into the waves," Sean went on, continuing to rub the wax into the pink-striped board. "Surfers spend most of their time paddling, Liz."

"Sounds like fun," Elizabeth teased. "But you must get to stand up for a few seconds."

"Sure, eventually. But *you* won't be standing up for a while," Sean continued, laughing. "Standing up on a surfboard looks a whole lot easier than it is. Today I just want you to ride on your knees to get the feel of the waves and the board."

Elizabeth was secretly relieved. As Sean spoke, Elizabeth found herself glancing uneasily at the ocean, watching the waves roll in to shore. If she had to do it on those gigantic waves, even riding on her knees seemed pretty scary. For a moment she considered backing out, telling Sean she had made a terrible mistake. No one would ever know the difference, and she could go on being Miss Conservative for the rest of her life.

Come on, Liz, she told herself. *Aren't you trying to be more daring? You came out here to prove a point, so prove it!*

"OK, Liz," Sean exclaimed, throwing the wax into his bag. "Let's hit the water!"

Elizabeth's heart was pounding as she knelt on the surfboard and paddled farther and farther out into the waves. Sean assured her that the surf was not that big, but the waves seemed huge to her.

She tried to concentrate on Sean's instructions. *Paddle out to a good wave, turn around and face the shore, catch the swell, and then turn to your left and slide along the wave.* Finally she got up the nerve, turned her board toward the shore, and felt herself rising on a wave. But suddenly her mind went blank, and she forgot what she was supposed to do. She panicked as the wave grew under her. A moment later the water crashed over her, and Elizabeth toppled into the water.

She came up gasping for breath and grabbed her board, which was floating beside her.

"Are you all right, Liz?" Sean shouted from shore through his cupped hands.

Elizabeth raised her arm in response.

"Great. You forgot to turn to the left and slide along the wave," he called out in a calm, assuring voice. "Why don't you try again, and this time don't forget to *turn to the left*."

"All right," Elizabeth called, trying to sound confident. But she was even more nervous for her second try than she was for her first.

"And you'd better not wipe out again. You've got an audience now!" Sean called.

Elizabeth looked off to the beach and saw Sammy, Dave, and Laurie standing next to Sean. When Sammy and Dave waved at her, she gave a little shy wave in return, then felt a rush of nervous energy. *This time I'm going to do it right*, she thought, setting her jaw.

She paddled out farther, caught sight of the perfect wave, and turned to shore. *Remember to turn to the left and slide along the wave*, she reminded herself, looking over her shoulder at the approaching whitecap.

I'll be happy to stay on my knees for this ride! she thought as she felt the swell lift her board. The power of the crashing wave rose behind her, and Elizabeth could hear its roar.

"Turn left!" Sean shouted at her.

She paddled desperately to the left, and then suddenly she felt her board dip gracefully down and go sliding along the wave. It took a moment for her to realize what was happening.

She was surfing! She couldn't believe it.

The ride seemed to go on forever. Elizabeth was sure she had been kneeling on the board for five full minutes when the wave finally tossed her from the surfboard. But this time she came up laughing, and paddled toward shore.

Sammy, Dave, Sean, and Laurie were all standing together, clapping, as Elizabeth emerged from the surf.

"Nice ride!" Sammy exclaimed as Elizabeth approached. "I give you a perfect ten for form."

"So does Sean," Dave muttered, just loud enough for Elizabeth to hear. He jabbed Sean playfully in the ribs.

"That was a great job, Liz!" Sean exclaimed. He reached around her and gave her a hug.

"It wasn't *that* great of a ride," Elizabeth said as she quickly pulled away, a little shocked.

"But you were up for almost fifteen seconds," Sean responded.

"Fifteen seconds?" Elizabeth cried. "It felt more like fifteen minutes!"

"It always does at first," Sammy added. "But believe me, fifteen seconds is a *great* first ride."

"Even on my knees?" Elizabeth asked.

"Even on your knees," Sammy assured her.

"Now let's see *you* ride a wave, Sean," Laurie said. "I've always heard that the best teachers teach by example."

"Come on, Mr. Big Surfing Teacher," Dave added. "Show your prize student how it's *really* done."

"If you *insist*." Sean grinned and bounded off into the water.

Elizabeth walked over to Laurie and watched Sean paddle out.

"Are you a surfer, too, Laurie?" Elizabeth asked.

"No," Laurie answered. "I just hang around the clubhouse."

"You should give it a try sometime," Elizabeth said, still excited from her ride. "It's a terrific thrill."

"I love watching Sean surf," Laurie said. "He's the best."

Just then, Sean began a beautiful ride along a

huge white wave. He crouched down into a graceful curl and held his arms out for balance. Suddenly Sean began walking toward the nose of the board.

"What's he doing?" Elizabeth asked.

"Hotdogging," Laurie said, smiling.

"Not bad," Sammy said coolly, checking out Sean's form.

"Not bad at all," Dave replied. "He's going to try to hang ten."

"What's that?" Elizabeth asked, gazing out at Sean with rapt attention.

"Only the most difficult stunt in surfing," Dave answered.

Sean had moved to the very tip of the surfboard. In fact, Elizabeth noticed Sean was so far forward that his toes curled over the edge of the board. He was squatting down low, just under the curl of the cresting wave.

"He's hanging ten!" Laurie cried.

"I don't think I'll try *that* for a while," Elizabeth said to Laurie.

Laurie laughed. "Me, either—I mean, I'd never have the guts to do what Sean does. He's incredible."

"You sound like a big fan of his," Elizabeth commented.

"Yeah, well, I guess so. I've known him for years," Laurie answered.

"How nice!" Elizabeth exclaimed. "So, are you guys a couple?"

Laurie hesitated, shifting a little in the sand. "Uh, sort of. Like I said," she answered at last, "we've known each other for a long time."

Elizabeth breathed a little sigh of relief. As long as Sean was spoken for, she wouldn't have to worry about his flirtatiousness. *Some boys are just like that*, she thought. *And some girls, too!* Jessica immediately came to mind.

Sean emerged from the surf with his board under his arm and looked at Elizabeth with a triumphant expression. "Not bad, huh, Liz?" Sean said, coming closer.

"Pretty amazing, Sean," Elizabeth answered, turning to Laurie. But Laurie was walking quickly away.

That's strange, Elizabeth thought. *Why doesn't she want to see Sean?*

"Enough entertainment," Sean said, patting Elizabeth on the shoulder. "Now get back out there and get to work!"

When practice was over for the day, Elizabeth said goodbye to Sean and headed over to the ice cream parlor on the beach. She was starved after such a long and difficult workout. Her knees hurt from crouching on the board, and she had fallen into the water more times than she could count.

I feel like I'm training for a triathlon, she thought. *But at least I'm doing something different.*

34

Elizabeth felt she deserved a triple scoop with extra chocolate sprinkles, but she settled for a small cone, since she would be heading home for dinner soon. She didn't want to surprise everyone with how fat she could get!

She handed the boy a dollar and walked back onto the beach and dropped down in the sand. As she licked the ice cream, Elizabeth gazed out at the rolling waves. She was enjoying surfing a lot more than she thought she would. It was scary but thrilling.

Elizabeth saw a girl over to her right riding a surfboard on her knees, just as she had earlier. Only this girl wasn't having very much success. It didn't look as if she had a teacher, either. For a minute Elizabeth thought the surfer was Laurie. But that was impossible: she said she didn't surf.

It must be someone who looks like Laurie, she decided as she stood up to leave. *Well, time to get back to being plain old Elizabeth!*

The next afternoon Jessica was having a malt with Lila in the Dairi Burger. She had called Lila and demanded that she meet her for a top-secret discussion.

"This wouldn't have anything to do with Caroline Pearce, would it?" Lila asked.

"You'd better believe it does," Jessica cried.

"Listen to this. Last night Caroline Pearce borrowed her parents' new car. Her parents are out of town, and Caroline is under strict orders *not* to drive the car. So guess what happened?"

"She got a parking ticket?" Lila suggested, looking decidedly bored.

"No," Jessica said, ignoring Lila's tone. "She took out the car and put a big fat *dent* in the fender and scratched the side. And now she has to earn all the money for the repairs. And guess how she's doing that?"

"How?" Lila asked.

"She's got a job at the Unique Boutique, that new shop in the mall. And I've come up with a great plan to get back at her for spreading rumors about me." Jessica leaned back and crossed her arms. "But *I* need your help." She knew Lila couldn't resist being devious when given the chance.

Lila smiled. "Just tell me what to do."

"Well, you'll be the decoy," Jessica said. "All you have to do is buy a scarf or two."

"I don't get it," Lila said, leaning closer to Jessica.

"OK, here's the plan," Jessica began, lowering her voice to a conspiratorial whisper. "I'm going to start spending a whole lot of time shopping in the Unique Boutique. And not only that, but I'm going to become the most *demanding* customer in the world. I mean the kind of customer that salespeople have nightmares about. And what can Caroline Pearce do about it? *Nothing!* Because she has to be nice and sweet to every single customer, or else she'll lose her job. And believe me, Caroline *needs* this job. The car repairs are going to cost a lot."

Jessica and Lila broke out in peals of laughter.

"You are *terrible*, Jessica Wakefield!" Lila managed between laughs.

"And all you have to do," Jessica continued, "is buy a scarf or a pair of earrings every once in a while, so the boss doesn't get suspicious."

"I think I can handle that," Lila remarked with a sly smile. "I need some new earrings anyway."

"Great," Jessica said excitedly. "We'll start on Friday, right after school. This is going to be so much fun!"

Four

On Thursday, right after school, Elizabeth was back at Moon Beach, ready to try her first standing ride. As she paddled through the surf on her purple board, Elizabeth had a vision of herself standing right up and slicing gracefully through a wave, just like Sean had done.

"Remember not to try to stand up too *fast!*" Sean shouted from the beach. "Hey, Liz, are you listening? I said don't stand up too fast!"

But Elizabeth didn't really hear the words. Instead, she was thinking about how beautiful her first ride would be. Even though the competition was three weeks away, Elizabeth couldn't wait to show off in front of all her friends. They would be both shocked and amazed when they saw her ride a wave with utter perfection.

"Remember, Liz," Sean shouted, beginning to pace nervously around on the sand, "if your board pearls and you think it's flying above you, then *dive!* The ankle strap is long enough

38

for you to dive deep so you won't get hit. Got it, Liz?"

But Elizabeth had already caught sight of the perfect wave rolling toward her with a giant swell and a foamy white crest. She turned her board toward the shore and felt the exhilarating lift as the wave caught her from behind.

What a thrill. Just as on her first ride, Elizabeth felt the board begin to slide effortlessly along the wave. Now all she had to do was get to her feet.

She jumped up and planted her feet on the speeding surfboard. She knew something had gone wrong, but she couldn't figure out what it was. She felt the board dip down a little, and then the tip sank beneath the water. The next thing she knew, the board shot out from under her and went soaring up into the air. She tumbled into the water, and just as she was rising to the surface she felt a *whack!*—right on her rear end.

Back on shore, Sean was waiting for her with his arms crossed, smiling and tapping his foot. "OK, Miss Hot Dog," he began, sounding like a cross schoolteacher. "Now, would you please tell me what you did wrong?"

"I guess I thought I was a better surfer than I am," Elizabeth replied, struggling out of the water with her surfboard. "Can you believe I was actually thinking about hanging ten?"

"Liz," Sean began, looking at Elizabeth with admiring eyes, "I surfed for a whole summer before I even *thought* about hanging ten. You're really an adventurous girl."

"You think so?" she wondered out loud.

"I do *now*," Sean said, spreading some sun cream on his muscular shoulders. "But when I first saw you, I had you pegged as just another good-looking scaredy-cat."

"Really?" Elizabeth said, blushing. *So I even look wimpy*, she thought to herself.

"But now that you're not a scaredy-cat," Sean continued, putting a dab of cream on his fingers, "I guess that means you're just good-looking."

Elizabeth wished Sean wouldn't spend so much of the lesson flirting with her. But now that she knew he was going out with Laurie, at least she could tell he wasn't being serious.

"I guess I screwed up that ride, didn't I?" Elizabeth said, anxious to change the subject.

"But you were punished for it," Sean responded, sending Elizabeth a teasing smirk.

"What do you mean?" Elizabeth asked, already feeling the blush creeping up her neck.

"I noticed that the surfboard gave you a pretty good spanking!" Sean chuckled.

Elizabeth felt her cheeks burning.

"You're OK, aren't you?" Sean asked, peering around Elizabeth. "Just a bruised—"

"Ego!" Elizabeth interjected, turning quickly toward the waves again before Sean could notice how red she was.

This time when Elizabeth paddled out, she kept in mind everything Sean had told her. And when she caught her next wave, she stood up very slowly and very carefully. The board felt a little unsteady beneath her, but she was pretty sure she could keep it under control. She glanced over her back and saw the white crest of the wave curling toward her. The board seemed to speed along without any effort. And she had been riding for ten whole seconds before it finally dawned on her: she was actually standing up and surfing!

But just then, the wave crested and crashed into her, and Elizabeth went sprawling into the water.

"You did it, Liz, you did it!" Sean cried as Elizabeth climbed out of the surf. "I knew you could."

"That was great!" Elizabeth exclaimed. "I felt like I was flying."

Sean gave her a few more tips—especially on ways to stop a ride without wiping out each time—and then sent Elizabeth back into the surf. On her next few rides, she became more and more steady on her feet. Sean called out directions from the beach.

When Sean and Elizabeth finally headed toward

the clubhouse, Elizabeth glanced down at her watch. She couldn't believe her eyes. The lesson was only supposed to be an hour long, but nearly two hours had flown by. She was exhausted, but she couldn't help but smile happily to herself as she carried her surfboard across the beach.

"I hope it's OK that the lesson went a little late today," Sean said as he replaced Elizabeth's board in the rack at the clubhouse. "I mean, I hope you didn't have any other plans or anything."

"I totally lost track of the time," Elizabeth replied, tossing her wax into her knapsack. "But I didn't have any plans anyway."

"Oh, really?" Sean's eyes lit up, and he opened his mouth to speak, but Elizabeth cut him off.

"Sean, who do you think was the greatest surfer ever?" she asked. "And why?"

"Bob Simmons, no doubt," Sean said. "Simmons was the greatest."

"Why?" Elizabeth asked, slipping her shorts on over her swimsuit.

She could hardly believe she was as interested in surfing as she was. She had expected her new daring life to be difficult, but it wasn't at all. She smiled as she realized how much she had been missing.

"Bob Simmons lost the use of his left arm," Sean told her, "and he surfed with only one arm. Maybe he wasn't the best *surfer*, in terms of prizes and all that, but over thirty years ago he designed the kind of surfboard that we all still use today."

"Really?" Elizabeth asked.

"Yeah, it's incredible," Sean remarked. "In fact, the board *you* use is based on the design that Simmons came up with in the fifties. An original Simmons board is worth about five thousand dollars."

"Five thousand dollars?" Elizabeth gasped. "For a *surfboard?*"

"Not just any surfboard, a *Simmons*. And you know what?" Sean continued. "I actually *have* an original Simmons."

"Are you kidding?"

"No. I've got a pretty good collection of other rare boards, too. I keep them in the garage at home," Sean added. Suddenly a glimmer appeared in his eyes. "Hey, since you don't have any plans, would you like to come over and see them?"

Elizabeth hesitated, but just for a second. "Sure," she said. "The more I learn about surfing, the better I'll be, right?"

"Right," Sean agreed. "With that attitude, you'll be a pro in no time."

That's the plan, Elizabeth thought, grinning. *Elizabeth Wakefield, Surfing Champion*. "Let's go!"

* * *

The Blakes' garage was filled with beautiful, shining surfboards. Sean walked from board to board, giving Elizabeth the history of each one.

"What's that beautiful red one?" Elizabeth asked, pointing at a board in the corner.

"That's from the 1930s. It's a redwood surfboard, and it's *heavy*," Sean answered. "In fact, I'll bet you can barely pick it up."

"I'm sure glad you didn't give me *that* one to learn on," Elizabeth said.

"And here's the Simmons," Sean said.

"It's beautiful. You really have an amazing collection," Elizabeth remarked.

"Hey, Liz," Sean added. "Would you like to go inside and see some of my surfing trophies?"

"Thanks for the invitation, but—" Elizabeth started.

"Or maybe we could rent a movie for the VCR," Sean suggested eagerly.

Elizabeth got the feeling it was time for her to leave. Something suddenly seemed a little too personal, in a way she couldn't quite explain. Sean wasn't just flirting anymore; he really wanted to spend time with her. Elizabeth wasn't interested in Sean in any way other than as a teacher. She was about to tell Sean all about Todd when she remembered Laurie MacNeil. *He has a girlfriend*, she thought, relieved.

"So what do you say, Liz?" Sean asked again. "Do you want to come in?"

"It's nice of you to ask, Sean, but it's getting kind of late, and I should get home for dinner," Elizabeth said, starting to walk toward the door. "But I had a great lesson and learned a ton about surfing. Thanks!"

"See you Saturday, OK?" Sean called after her.

"Definitely!" Elizabeth replied as she got into the car.

"Todd called at three-thirty, four-thirty, and five-thirty," Mrs. Wakefield announced when Elizabeth walked into the kitchen. Alice Wakefield smiled at her daughter. "My guess is that Todd misses you," she added.

"I'm a little later than I thought I'd be," Elizabeth said. "I'll call him back in a second."

"You look tired, Liz," Mrs. Wakefield said. "Is this marine biology project strenuous?"

"It's pretty hard work, Mom," Elizabeth answered. "But I'm having the time of my life."

"Good, I'm glad," Mrs. Wakefield said. "But you'd better give that boyfriend of yours a call."

Elizabeth went upstairs and called Todd from her room.

"I tried to get you a couple of times this afternoon," Todd said. "That project seems to be taking up an awful lot of time."

"I did get kind of wrapped up in things today," Elizabeth admitted.

"Are turtle eggs such good company?" Todd teased. But Elizabeth could tell that he was a little jealous.

"You'll see what I've been so excited about pretty soon," she told him. Elizabeth didn't like to mislead Todd, or anyone else, for that matter. *But*, she thought, *I'm not really lying—I'm just not telling the whole truth.*

"You know what *I'm* excited about?" Todd asked. "Our date Saturday night. And if you tell me you have to do research that night, then I'll be *really* mad!"

"Of course I don't!" Elizabeth cried. She could tell Todd was only joking about being mad. "I can't wait for Saturday, either. But in the meantime, how about lunch tomorrow in the scenic Sweet Valley High cafeteria?"

"Table for two?" Todd asked.

"I'm not sure we'll be able to find one, but we can try!" Elizabeth said.

"Tell me all about it, Jess!" Amy exclaimed.

Jessica sat cross-legged on her unmade bed. Her room was so messy, it looked like a hurricane had just blown through.

"Caroline Pearce was just about ready to *explode!*" Jessica began, lying down on her bed and wriggling her feet. "She stood there and watched me take out every single sweater from the stack she had just straightened up. Amy, you should have seen the look on her face—she was ready to kill me! But there was nothing she could do because the manager was standing right there!"

"Did you buy anything?" Amy asked. "Or did you just terrorize her?"

"Are you kidding?" Jessica shrieked. "Even if I had found the coolest outfit in the world I wouldn't have bought it. But Lila got a pair of earrings. That way the manager saw us buying something, but Caroline didn't get the pleasure of taking any money from me."

"You've sure got all the bases covered, Jess," Amy said.

Jessica giggled. "There's no way Caroline can get herself out of *this* one."

Five

On Saturday afternoon Elizabeth climbed out of the surf with her board tucked under her arm, tired but exuberant. She smiled as she walked toward Sean. That afternoon she learned how to pull out of ride without wiping out. After three hilarious, disastrous attempts—when she went sprawling into the waves—Elizabeth finally pulled out perfectly and gracefully. As she made her way across the soft sand, Elizabeth felt the warm glow of triumph.

"Great lesson, Liz. You're a wonderful student!" Sean exclaimed. He handed Elizabeth a towel and kept talking as she dried her hair and tried to knock the water out of her ears.

"You've just got to remember to crouch down when you pull out," Sean continued, squatting down to demonstrate. "Because if you don't, you'll always wipe out."

"I think I've done enough wiping out to last a

lifetime." Elizabeth said. "What're you drawing there in the sand?"

"This is a diagram of the currents here at Moon Beach," Sean answered, pointing at the lines in the sand. "A surfer needs to know as much about currents and reefs and tides as any scientist. And an excellent surfer probably knows nearly as much about sea life as a marine biologist."

"Really?" Elizabeth asked, fascinated.

"We've been surfing to the right of the reef out there—" Sean began, pointing at his diagram and then out at the waves.

"We have?" Elizabeth interrupted. "How can you tell there's a reef?"

"Easy," Sean said. "You can tell by the way the waves are breaking. But you have to watch out when you're scouting out a new place to surf. You have to make sure you don't check it out at high tide, then find out at low tide that you've got some nasty reefs and riptides."

"I've been hearing about riptides for years, but you know, I've never known exactly what one is," Elizabeth said as the two of them headed across the sand toward the clubhouse.

"A riptide is a surface current of water running back to the sea from the shore," Sean answered. "And it's the thing that pulls surfers and swimmers far out into the ocean. If you've ever been caught in a riptide, you know how strong and frightening the ocean is. Let's put it this way, Liz," Sean added, a twinkle in his eye. "When you're dealing with a riptide, it doesn't matter how many laps you've done in your pool at home."

Elizabeth laughed. "No, I guess not."

"Hey, Liz," Sean said when they reached the clubhouse, "I was wondering if you'd like to go up to Jackson's Bluff with me this afternoon. It's the best place in Southern California to check out the tides and waves."

Elizabeth had heard of Jackson's Bluff, but the twinkle in Sean's eyes made her a little leery. "I should probably get home—before everyone starts wondering where I am," she said.

"But we still need to go over some important safety guidelines," Sean reminded her. "This way we can go over that stuff in the car on the way up."

Elizabeth didn't know what to do. She wanted to learn everything she could about surfing. But she was feeling a little guilty about all the time she was spending away from the other things she loved, like Enid, and her writing . . . and especially Todd.

"Come on, Liz," Sean said coaxingly. "We'll have fun. And there's so much more you need to know."

"I don't know how you do it, Sean," Elizabeth responded, "but you've convinced me again."

"Great! I'll drive," Sean said, smiling.

Laurie stood at the clubhouse window and watched Elizabeth climb into Sean's Jeep. When the car turned and headed north, Laurie was somehow *sure* that Sean was taking Elizabeth up to Jackson's Bluff, the spot where all the Big Mesa kids went when they wanted to be alone. Sadly, she watched them disappear up the road.

"Did Sean tell you where he was going, Laurie?" Sammy asked from behind the counter. "He's supposed to close up the clubhouse tonight."

"No, he didn't," Laurie answered quietly, still gazing out the window. "He was with Elizabeth."

Sammy lifted his eyebrows. "They've sure been spending a lot of extra time together. He blew off work on Thursday and took Elizabeth over to his house to show her his surfboard collection."

Laurie felt her heart sink. All of her worst fears seemed to be coming true. "See you later, Sammy. I'm going home," Laurie said glumly.

"Later!" Sammy called out as Laurie left the clubhouse.

Sean barely even said hello to me today, Laurie thought as she headed toward her car. *We used to hang out all the time, and now he acts as if I don't exist.*

Well, at least there's something I can still try, she thought. She started the car and pulled out of the parking lot. Laurie had been practicing her surfing at a beach just north of Moon Beach. The first few times she had surfed, she had been afraid that someone she knew would see her—she knew that she surfed terribly. She liked the other beach because she could be alone when she wanted to, but there were also some friendly girls there who helped her learn the more difficult moves. Already she could understand Sean's fascination with the sport. It was exhilarating, and it required intense concentration.

She drove up to Crescent Beach and parked the car. It was time to hit the waves!

Jackson's Bluff jutted high above a wild stretch of ocean. Sean pulled his Jeep right up to the edge of the bluff, where there was a fantastic view.

"Now, look at that patch of white waves out there in the middle," Sean began, pointing out toward the water. "What does that mean?"

"Is this a quiz?" Elizabeth asked, chuckling.

"You'd better believe it," Sean said.

"Well, all those little breakers must mean that there's a reef under there," Elizabeth answered.

"A-plus!" Sean cried.

Sean proceeded to tell Elizabeth all about coral reefs and ocean currents and marine life. As he talked he leaned over close to Elizabeth and pointed out at the waves.

"When you want to find a secluded place to surf, you just look for breaking waves," Sean said.

"Like those over there?" Elizabeth asked, pointing at some whitecaps.

"No," Sean answered, taking Elizabeth's hand and pointing it in another direction. "Like those waves right there."

"Oh, I see them now," Elizabeth answered.

But Sean kept holding Elizabeth's hand. A moment passed, and Elizabeth held her breath.

"That's all it takes to discover a nice, quiet, secluded place where you can go surfing with one special person," Sean added. At last he took his hand away, and Elizabeth breathed a sigh of relief.

He must be thinking of Laurie, Elizabeth realized.

"There are some beaches farther north that you and I can go to sometime," Sean said.

"I think I'd better just learn how to surf on Moon Beach first!" Elizabeth laughed.

"Well, maybe you're right, Liz," Sean began,

lifting his eyebrows. "At least Moon Beach doesn't get too many sharks."

"Sharks!" Elizabeth cried. "What do you mean by *too many*?"

"Well, what I mean is that no one's been *killed* by a shark there yet," Sean added, grinning.

"Have you been letting me go out in shark-infested waters?" Elizabeth exclaimed, her face suddenly pale.

"Well, it's not as bad as some other places," Sean answered playfully. "If we were to go surfing here at Jackson's Bluff, we'd not only have to worry about sharks, but we'd also have to watch out for sea urchins and barnacles and jellyfish and sharp mussels and—"

"Enough!" Elizabeth said, covering her face with her hands. "Do you want me to quit surfing altogether, before the big competition?"

"You'd better not, Liz," Sean warned.

"You're only saying that because you don't want to lose the bet and have to spend three months working weekends."

"That's not true, and you know it," Sean responded. "Of course I want you to do well in the competition. But mostly I've enjoyed just being with you."

"It *has* been kind of fun," Elizabeth added quickly, feeling a little uncomfortable again. "And I can't believe how much I like surfing. Oh, you know what, Sean?" Elizabeth checked her watch.

"I think it's time for me to go. Could you drive me back to my car now?"

"So soon?" Sean asked. "But I wanted to—"

"Give me another test?" Elizabeth joked. "Go ahead—ask me anything about surfing." *Just don't ask me out tonight*, she added silently.

Elizabeth strolled into the kitchen as the Wakefields were getting ready for dinner. Ned Wakefield, the twins' handsome, broad-shouldered father, was standing at the counter carving the meat while Mrs. Wakefield scooped beans into a serving dish. Jessica, being Jessica, was gabbing on the telephone.

"Hello, Liz," Mr. Wakefield said as he lowered his cheek to Elizabeth's kiss.

"Hi, Dad!" Elizabeth said. "What's new with you?"

"Well, let's see," Mr. Wakefield began. "Pretty much the same old lawyer stuff, Liz. But come to think of it, we did get a case today that you might be interested in."

"What's that?" Elizabeth asked as she began removing plates from the cabinet to set the table. It was actually Jessica's night to set the table, but considering the squeals of laughter coming from the direction of the telephone, Elizabeth guessed she might starve before Jessica even thought of the table. And after all of her surfing, Elizabeth was absolutely famished.

"The case involves a young man, a professional surfer, who drowned last year after being dragged out to sea in a riptide," Mr. Wakefield began. "His family is suing because there weren't any signs on this beach warning people about the danger of riptides."

Elizabeth almost dropped a plate. "That's awful," she commented.

"I don't want to think about it!" Mrs. Wakefield exclaimed. "Not after what we went through with Jessica."

Mrs. Wakefield was referring to the time a charter boat capsized in a storm, and Jessica—along with Winston Egbert—was missing at sea for a whole day. It turned out Jessica had swum to a nearby island, and while everyone at home was praying she hadn't drowned, Jessica was lying on a beautiful beach, working on her tan.

Elizabeth felt guilty about keeping secrets from her parents. *But life is made up of taking risks, isn't it?* Elizabeth thought. And she *was* being as safe as possible when she surfed. She had a teacher who always watched out for her, too.

During dinner Elizabeth ate quickly, not only because she was hungry, but also because she had to hurry and get ready for her date with

Todd. As soon as she could, she excused herself from the table and rushed upstairs.

She was standing at the bathroom mirror getting ready when Jessica walked up and stood in the doorway.

"What are you doing tonight?" Jessica asked.

"Todd and I have a date," Elizabeth answered.

"I know *that*. Where are you going?"

"To that new French movie that's playing downtown." Elizabeth brushed her hair back from her face and fastened it into a ponytail.

"Figures," Jessica said, making a face. "Hey, you know, you've really been getting a good tan working on this biology project."

"Really?" Elizabeth said. "I hadn't noticed."

"You were probably too busy sifting through seaweed or something." Jessica giggled. "Maybe this project isn't such a bad thing after all, though. Are there any cute scientists up there?"

"Well, my lab partner *is* pretty good-looking," Elizabeth said, playing along. *And Sean is the type of guy Jessica would really like. If he weren't already going with Laurie, I might try to fix them up*, Elizabeth thought.

"Maybe I should go up there with you one day," Jessica said.

"I don't think so, Jess. It's pretty boring—you know, counting turtle eggs and stuff like that." Elizabeth shrugged, then began to apply some eyeliner. "Besides, I think he has a girlfriend."

"It figures. You know, I don't understand how you can be interested in that boring stuff and still be related to me." Jessica shook her head.

"Thanks a lot, Jess!" Elizabeth jabbed her sister in the ribs with her hairbrush. "I'm glad you think I'm so dull."

Just then, the door bell rang downstairs.

"That's Todd. How do I look?" Elizabeth asked. "No, don't tell me—I don't want to hear how boring my outfit is."

"Come on, Liz, you know I don't mean it," Jessica said. "But if you did want to borrow something . . . say, my leopard-print skirt?" She grinned.

"No, thanks," Elizabeth said, laughing as she ran down the stairs. "See you later!"

"I must admit, Liz, I've been pretty jealous of this extra-credit project," Todd said as he drove toward downtown Sweet Valley. "I mean, you're the last person in the world who needs extra credit," he added.

"I know, but I'm really excited about it," Elizabeth said. "We're doing some interesting research. And the reason I can't tell you about it is that there's going to be a big presentation at the end of the month, up at the Marine Biology

Center on Moon Beach. And I want you to be my guest of honor."

"I'm thrilled," Todd said, rolling his eyes. "At least now I have a *biology* presentation to look forward to."

"You may be surprised," Elizabeth said, tapping her fingers nervously against the car door. She wanted so much to tell Todd everything. She hated to see him jealous and grumpy. But, on the other hand, she wanted her surfing debut to be a complete shock to everyone. "It may not be as boring as you think," Elizabeth added.

"Let's not talk about your project anymore, or even *think* about it, OK?" Todd said.

"Hey, I've got a good idea," Elizabeth said, turning to Todd. "Why don't we skip the movie and drive out to the beach? There's a full moon, Todd."

"This wouldn't have anything to do with your marine biology project, would it?" Todd asked.

"Don't be silly," Elizabeth remarked. "I just think it would be nice to look at the ocean in the moonlight with you."

Todd agreed, and a few minutes later they pulled up onto a bluff overlooking the ocean. As soon as Elizabeth settled into Todd's arms, she knew it had been too long since they had been together and spent a quiet evening, with nothing to do but kiss and talk.

But even though Elizabeth was happy to be

with Todd, she kept glancing out the window to catch a view of the waves in the moonlight. She couldn't help but notice how the surf was breaking and whether the tide was in or out. The moonlight glittered romantically on the water, but Elizabeth was imagining how far out she would paddle and where she could catch the best waves . . .

"You're so quiet," Todd observed. "What are you thinking about?"

"Oh," Elizabeth said, surprised. "Nothing." *Nothing I can tell you now, that is.*

"Are you sure?" Todd asked, sounding a little suspicious.

"Actually, I was thinking about how nice it feels to be here with you," Elizabeth replied.

Todd pulled her closer to him. "Same here."

Six

"We'll catch the next one!" Sean cried, paddling his surfboard through the waves, his strong, tanned shoulders flexing. "The one cresting just now!"

It was ten days later, and Elizabeth had had three more lessons. She had made a lot of progress, and now Sean wanted her to try surfing the same wave with him.

"Looks like a beauty!" Elizabeth cried in response. She was paddling twenty feet across from Sean, just managing to keep up with him.

"Now, remember, Liz," Sean called out across the waves, "try to keep your speed up so I don't run into you!"

"Are you sure I'm ready for this?" Elizabeth yelled.

"We'll find out, won't we?" Sean said, turning his board toward the shore. "Get ready, here she comes!"

Elizabeth turned her board toward the shore

and then felt the familiar list of the cresting swell. Over the past couple of weeks, she had come to know these things very well, and now she could almost say she was a "real" surfer. Not as good as Sean—not even *close*—but still, she knew that after only six lessons, she was doing pretty well.

Her heart was pounding with excitement as she rose from her knees to her feet. Sean was riding the same wave right behind her, and a moment later she heard him yell, "Yahoo!"

She glanced over her shoulder and caught a glimpse of Sean surfing just behind her, white sea spray flying up all around him. He had a huge grin on his handsome face.

"Don't look back at me or you'll wipe out!" Sean yelled.

"Am I going fast enough?!" Elizabeth screamed.

"Just perfect!" Sean responded. "Now hold steady while I sneak up a little."

Sean slid forward along the wave toward Elizabeth, until he could almost have reached out and touched her. Then he let out another excited yelp.

Elizabeth glanced over her shoulder again, and when she caught Sean's eye, he winked at her. Before she knew it, the nose of her surfboard dipped under the wave, and she went flying into the water.

Her board flew up and hit Sean's board, and he went sprawling into the waves beside her.

They both came up unhurt, laughing and sputtering, and retrieved their surfboards.

"I *told* you not to look back at me!" Sean cried as they paddled toward shore.

"Well, nothing would have happened if you hadn't *winked* at me!" Elizabeth responded.

"I couldn't help it," Sean answered, grinning. "You looked so beautiful out there."

Elizabeth tried to ignore Sean's comment as they headed toward the clubhouse.

"Our lessons are halfway over, Liz," Sean said as he put their surfboards away. "And I think you're doing *great*. You have a lot of natural talent."

"Really?" Elizabeth asked. "You're not just saying that to be nice?"

"Are you kidding?" Sean said. "Most people don't even *try* to stand up after six lessons, and here we are, already riding the same wave. It's incredible!"

Elizabeth smiled. "I must admit, I've really been enjoying these lessons. I even surprised myself with how much fun I've been having. I can't wait to surprise all my friends at the competition."

Sean shifted a little and looked down shyly at his feet. "Speaking of the big competition, Liz," he began, "I want you to know that I don't really care about this bet. I don't mind working weekends. I just don't want you to feel any pressure or anything."

"That's sweet of you, Sean," Elizabeth responded.

"But on the other hand, Liz," Sean continued, grinning slyly, "I fully *expect* that my expert teaching will have made you into a total surf goddess by then. In fact, I wouldn't be surprised if you walk away with a first-place trophy!"

"Flattery will get you nowhere, Mr. Blake," Elizabeth teased. "But I must admit, I do feel lucky to have you as my teacher."

"Believe me, Liz," Sean responded, looking directly into Elizabeth's eyes, "I feel lucky, too. Hey, can I buy you a soda?"

"I should really go . . ." Elizabeth began.

"Relax a little. You had a tough workout today." He opened the clubhouse refrigerator and set a soda on the counter for Elizabeth. Sean sat down on a ragged old couch, and Elizabeth took the soda and sat down beside him.

"OK," Elizabeth said, "but just for a few minutes. I've got a ton of homework to do tonight."

"A few minutes is all I need," Sean remarked coyly.

"What do you mean?"

Just then, Sean reached into his canvas bag and pulled out a small, prettily wrapped white package. "I have something for you. In honor of your dedication to surfing."

"Oh, Sean! That's so nice of you," Elizabeth cried, carefully opening the present. "But you didn't have to."

"I know," Sean answered. "I *wanted* to."

Elizabeth lifted the lid of the box and pulled out a layer of cotton. Sitting in the bottom of the box was a tiny silver charm in the shape of a surfboard. "This is great," Elizabeth said. "I haven't gotten a new charm in a long time."

Before she knew what was happening, Sean wrapped his arms around her waist. Then he turned his face toward hers, as if he wanted to kiss her. She put her hand on his chest and gently, but firmly, pushed him away.

"Liz," Sean muttered, "I thought you—"

"You thought I what?" Elizabeth asked.

"I thought you liked me," Sean answered.

"I *do* like you, Sean," Elizabeth assured him gently. "But what about Laurie?"

Sean looked at her, a puzzled expression on his face. "Do you mean Laurie MacNeil? What about her?"

"I thought she was your girlfriend," Elizabeth replied.

"Laurie MacNeil?" Sean cried. "Oh, no. Laurie and I have been pals since we were little kids, there's definitely nothing romantic happening between us. I mean, we had a date a couple of weeks ago, but . . ."

"But what?" Elizabeth asked.

"But I've never really been interested in anyone like I am in you," he said, looking hopefully at Elizabeth.

"Sean, I have a serious boyfriend," Elizabeth began. "We've been together a long time."

"Oh," Sean said sadly.

"It wouldn't be fair to lead you on," she continued. "I know that we have a lot of fun together, and I know that our time is usually pretty intense, but there's nothing romantic in it for me."

"I feel like a jerk," Sean said.

"Don't feel like a jerk," Elizabeth said, "because *I* sure don't think you're one."

"I guess you'll probably want to stop coming to the lessons," Sean said. "Now that I've made a major league idiot out of myself."

Elizabeth shook her head. "Not at all. I came here to learn how to surf, and you're the best one to teach me. And I *definitely* want us to stay friends."

Sean looked disappointed, but he also seemed to accept what Elizabeth was saying. Elizabeth picked up the little box and held it out to Sean. "Here," she quietly, "I don't know if I feel right about accepting this now."

"Please keep it, Liz," Sean responded, trying

to smile. "It might bring you good luck in the competition."

"Are you sure?" Elizabeth asked, still holding the box out to him.

"Of course I'm sure," Sean said quietly. "And maybe the charm will work for me, too."

"Sean," Elizabeth began, with a firmness in her voice, "I don't want you to hope that things will change between us. I really *do* love my boyfriend."

"You can't stop a guy from dreaming, can you?" Sean said, then laughed good-naturedly. "Don't worry, Liz. I know *I* just wiped out in a major way. I won't hassle you at all—except about the finer details of surfing. Promise."

Elizabeth nodded, grateful that Sean understood. "Thanks. See you Thursday?"

"Sure thing," Sean agreed. "Same time, same place."

Laurie MacNeil had been walking up to the clubhouse to visit Sean when she heard her name. She stopped and listened to the voices that were drifting out the clubhouse's open window.

"Laurie MacNeil!" Sean said. "There's definitely nothing romantic happening between us."

Laurie felt the hot tears filling her eyes. She had tried to keep them from falling, but then she heard Sean's voice continue: "But I've never really been interested in anyone like I am in you."

All of Laurie's worst fears were coming true. She had *known* that Sean would fall for Elizabeth Wakefield! And now her chances of winning Sean's heart were smaller than ever. She ran across the parking lot, got into her car, put her face in her hands, and cried.

Now, just as she was drying her eyes, she saw Elizabeth walk toward her red Fiat carrying a small white box. *Sean has never given me anything,* she thought, and the tears began again.

But by the time she had calmed down again, Laurie had made a decision. What did she need from Sean Blake, anyway? All he was doing was causing her a lot of pain. *I'm going to give him a piece of my mind!* she thought. She took a deep breath, got out of the car, and marched across the sandy lot to the clubhouse.

"Hello, Sean," she said as calmly as she could.

"Hi, Laurie," Sean said as he put a box of sun cream in the display case. His nose was covered with white zinc oxide, which made his green eyes sparkle. He glanced up and gave her a little smile. "How's work over at the ice cream parlor?" Sean asked.

"Fine," Laurie replied.

"Liz and I rode the same wave today," Sean continued, straightening the canisters of wax in the case. "She's getting to be a pretty good surfer. And the best thing is that she's so *interested* in surfing."

"Really?" Laurie asked.

"You know something?" Sean said. "*You* should try surfing."

"What makes you say that?" Laurie asked.

"You've always been a good athlete," Sean said. "Remember when we started up that neighborhood softball league in sixth grade? You were the star."

"Oh, yeah," Laurie said, smiling despite her resolve to stay angry with Sean. "That was fun."

"And remember last year when our class went canoeing and you were the only one who didn't turn over in the rapids?" Sean continued. "You could probably be an OK surfer. But I guess you're just not interested."

"Oh, I don't know about that," Laurie mumbled as she turned to leave. "See you soon, Sean." Outside, she ran across the parking lot and hopped into her car.

Somehow all of her anger had vanished. The only thing she wanted to do now was to go home, get her board, and practice surfing until the sun set!

"Are you ready for your crash course in boutique terrorism?" Jessica asked as she and Amy drove toward the Sweet Valley Mall. It was Amy's first trip to the Unique Boutique, and Jessica couldn't wait to show her friend how she was repaying Caroline for her treachery.

"There are special techniques that take many hours of practice to perfect," Jessica added.

Amy smiled. "What sort of special techniques are you talking about?"

"For instance, how to pretend you're being incredibly nice while you're actually being the biggest pain in the world, or how to try on every color of a certain shirt without buying it. . . ."

"Sounds great to me!" Amy exclaimed.

"But I've got something extra special planned for today's campaign," Jessica announced, quickly pulling the Fiat into a parking space. "Follow me!"

Once inside the mall, Jessica bought a soda at Casey's Ice Cream Parlor. Then she walked into the Unique Boutique, ignoring the sign on the door that warned: No Food or Drink Allowed.

Caroline Pearce threw a poisonous glance at Jessica, but Jessica ignored her. She and Amy made a big show of fumbling through piles of neatly stacked stone-washed jeans, but Caroline just watched them, standing behind the counter with her arms crossed. That was perfectly fine with Jessica. She knew that Caroline would have to clean up the mess anyway. After a few minutes, the whole jeans section was in total disarray.

Just then, the floor manager, a woman with a mean face, yelled, "Hey, Caroline, don't you see those two customers who need help? And when you're done, clean up this mess, too."

Jessica felt a twinge of guilt—ever so small—about how miserable she was making Caroline's life. Not only did Caroline have to suffer through her attacks, but she also had to put up with that terrible manager. But the twinge of guilt didn't last long when she remembered how humiliated she felt whenever someone at school called her Magenta Galaxy. *In fact*, she thought, watching Caroline storm toward her, *Caroline Pearce deserves whatever she gets*.

"I'm sorry, miss," Caroline said, pointing at the cup of soda in Jessica's hand. "Drinks are not allowed in the store."

"Oh, I'm sorry," Jessica responded sweetly. "Maybe you could throw it away for me."

But as Caroline reached for the cup, Jessica knocked it against Caroline's hand, and the drink spilled on the sleeve of Caroline's white blouse.

Jessica gasped. "I'm so sorry, Caroline!"

Amy began to laugh and covered her mouth with her hand.

"I've had just about enough of you, *miss!*" Caroline yelled, her face turning almost as red as her hair. And then she added, "Oh, I think I remember your name. Isn't it Magenta Galaxy?"

At that, Jessica's face suddenly went as red as Caroline's. "No, it's *not*," Jessica said, loud enough for the manager to hear, "and I'd appreciate getting some service in this store that isn't *rude*!"

"Is there a problem here?" the manager asked, approaching the girls quickly.

"Your salesgirl is calling me names," Jessica said.

"She is? I'm very sorry, miss," the manager said, turning to Caroline. "When you're finished stacking these clothes, Caroline, I'd like to have a word with you in my office."

Caroline tried to say something, but she was speechless with rage.

"And why are you wearing that shirt with a stain on the sleeve?" the manager added. "Is that any way to impress our customers?"

"No, ma'am," Jessica heard Caroline mumble as she and Amy walked out into the mall.

Outside the store, the two girls collapsed in utter hysterics.

"Did you see the look on Caroline's face?" Jessica roared with laughter.

"Even I was surprised when you spilled the drink," Amy cried. "I would never have had the guts to do that."

"It *was* a little bit mean, wasn't it?" Jessica said.

"Let's put it this way," Amy said. "If someone did that to *me*, I'd be plotting something big to return the favor!"

Jessica shook her head. "Caroline wouldn't dare. She knows she can't cross me again."

"Jess, you sound like someone in an old Western movie!" Amy joked.

"Come on, let's do some real shopping," Jessica said. "Speaking of Western, maybe I'll get a pair of cowboy boots!"

Seven

"Hello?" Elizabeth said as she picked up the phone on Thursday afternoon.

"Hi, Liz."

"Oh—hi, Sean. I think I know why you're calling."

"Yeah, this rain is a real bummer, isn't it?" Sean responded glumly. "I can't remember the last time it rained like this around here."

"Usually I love storms," Elizabeth said. "But not this one. There's only one week left to practice."

"I feel like a caged animal, sitting in this clubhouse with nobody around," Sean said. "If I knew any Indian rain dances, I'd do them backward to *stop* the rain."

"But can't we go surfing anyway?" Elizabeth asked. "I mean, we're going to get wet in the ocean, so why does it matter if it's raining?"

"Forget it, Liz," Sean said. "That huge storm last night made the ocean rough. And when the ocean gets rough, you get some serious riptides at Moon Beach. I might go out and surf in those waves, but I doubt you're ready for them."

Elizabeth sighed. "You're probably right."

"Let's just hope the rain stops soon," Sean said, a note of sadness in his voice. "But you could come to the clubhouse anyway, if you wanted. Just to keep me company."

"Thanks, Sean," Elizabeth responded, "but I think I'll use this free time to catch up on some things I've been neglecting."

"OK. Maybe I'll see you on Saturday, then. Pray for sun."

"Bye, Sean," Elizabeth said.

As soon as Sean hung up the phone, Elizabeth dialed Todd's number.

"Liz?" Todd said. "It's a surprise to hear from you."

"This storm has stopped work up at Moon Beach," Elizabeth explained, "and I was wondering if you'd like to come over for a rainy-day game of Scrabble."

"I don't know, Liz, I'm right in the middle of my homework," Todd began tentatively.

Since when can't Todd spare an hour from his homework to see me? Elizabeth wondered. *Maybe he's angrier than I thought.*

"But it's so nice to play games on rainy afternoons," Elizabeth added. "And I could make some hot chocolate while you're on your way."

"Well . . . OK," Todd said, his voice becoming a little cheerier. "I guess I *could* come over for a game or two."

"Great!" Elizabeth cried. "I can't wait to see you."

Elizabeth hung up, glad she had a chance to spend some time with Todd. Still, she wished she didn't have to miss a lesson. There was so little time left to practice before the big competition!

Elizabeth was already ahead by a hundred points in Scrabble. She and Todd were sitting on the carpet in the den, their mugs of hot chocolate half-finished beside them, while outside, the rain had begun to come down even harder.

It was Elizabeth's turn, and she put down the word *surfing*. She wanted to laugh and finally tell Todd what she was up to, but she couldn't— not yet.

"Not a bad word," Todd said. "But you've got to give me a chance—you're killing me!"

"I've just been lucky, Todd," Elizabeth responded.

"I think it helps that you're a writer, though," Todd added, laying his letters on the board. Then he pointed to the word he had just put down and laughed. "I mean, the best I can come up with is *jar*. How pathetic!"

"Yeah," Elizabeth answered vaguely.

She was thinking about the competition next Saturday and about all the surfing techniques Sean had taught her, and her mind wasn't really on the game at all. She was surprised she was winning when she was so distracted.

"I hear Jessica is giving Caroline a hard time over at the Unique Boutique," Todd said, a touch of impatience in his voice.

"Really," Elizabeth answered.

"I guess she's still angry about the story Caroline spread."

"Yeah," Elizabeth said flatly.

"Sometimes I feel a little bit sorry for Caroline, don't you?" Todd asked, tapping his fingers on the carpet.

"Yeah," Elizabeth said, placing her letters one by one on the board. Her word was *riptide*, and it landed on a triple word score.

Todd threw up his arms in frustration.

"I give up, Liz!" he cried.

"What's wrong?" Elizabeth asked, looking up and noticing the anger in Todd's face.

"I feel like you're a million miles away, that's what's wrong. I came over here to be with *you*, and you're hardly even here yourself."

Elizabeth sighed and looked sadly at Todd.

"We haven't been seeing each other enough to *begin* with," Todd continued, "and then when we *are* together, you're thinking about who

77

knows what—your stupid marine biology project or something."

"I'm sorry, Todd," Elizabeth said, "I guess I *am* concerned about my project."

"Well, I hope it's worth all this time and energy," Todd said shortly, getting up to leave.

"Hey, I've got an idea," Elizabeth cried, trying to salvage the afternoon. "Let's go to the Dairi Burger. I know I'll feel better after some fries and a malt."

"Are you sure you wouldn't rather be alone to think?" Todd asked angrily.

"Don't be silly!" Elizabeth stood up and grabbed Todd's hand. "I want to be with *you*."

"Well . . ." Todd said, his deep brown eyes softening a little. "Maybe just for a little while."

"Great!" Elizabeth said. She grabbed an umbrella and ran with Todd out through the pouring rain to his car.

Jessica and Lila entered the Unique Boutique, struggling with a huge load of fancy shopping bags. Caroline Pearce sent Jessica a withering look, but Jessica just smiled and nodded in return. She knew nothing would make Caroline angrier than a phony smile.

The girls' fancy bags were filled with dirty laundry, schoolbooks, and other things from home, but nobody had to know that.

"Now, you're sure you don't mind buying it?" Jessica quietly asked Lila as they walked toward the racks of expensive dresses.

"Not at all," Lila answered. "I think it's a *great* dress. Maybe a little bit expensive, but I can afford it."

"And it's all for a good cause," Jessica responded, winking at Lila.

Just then, the manager approached the girls.

"Good afternoon, ladies," she said. "May I help you?"

"Yes. I think my friend would like to buy this dress," Jessica answered, pointing to a sleek black linen sundress. She glanced over at Caroline and noticed that she was watching them distrustfully.

"Yes, I've had my eye on it for a long time," Lila remarked, "and I finally decided to buy it. A size six, please."

"Here we are, then," the manager said, taking the dress off the rack. "Would you like to try it on?"

"No," Lila said. "I'm sure it will fit."

"All right, then," the manager said, taking it toward the counter. I hope you can carry it. Judging from all your bags, you've already been on quite a shopping spree."

"I'm not so sure we *can* carry all of these bags," Jessica remarked wearily.

"Yeah, it would sure be a shame to drop something," Lila added with a tired sigh.

"Oh, I'm sure one of our salesgirls would be happy to help you carry your bags," the manager offered.

"That would be absolutely *perfect!*" Jessica cried, winking at Lila.

The manager pointed at Caroline. "She'd be delighted to help you," the manager said. "Will that be cash or charge?"

Lila paid in cash, and the woman wrapped the dress. A few minutes later, Jessica, Lila, and Caroline were standing beneath the roof of the mall's outdoor walkway, looking at the torrential rain. Jessica and Lila reached into their bags and pulled out their umbrellas. They opened them and started out into the parking lot.

Caroline hesitated, but a moment later she clamped her jaw and followed them into the rain. Jessica and Lila both looked back and saw that Caroline was already soaked, her red hair hanging flat against her forehead and neck. They both began giggling uncontrollably.

When Caroline got to the car, she dropped the bags into a puddle, gave Jessica another withering glance, then whirled around and ran back to the mall. Jessica and Lila scrambled into Lila's car, perfectly dry.

"She looked like a drowned rat!" Lila exclaimed.

"Mission accomplished!" Jessica said. "Let's go to the Dairi Burger and celebrate with a malt."

"Sounds perfect after a hard day's shopping," Lila remarked, laughing and pulling away in her car.

The Dairi Burger was packed with Sweet Valley High students. Todd and Elizabeth grabbed a free table near the door and sat down with an order of french fries and a malt. As she sipped the thick chocolate malt, Elizabeth felt her mood begin to brighten.

It's only a week until the big competition, and then Todd will understand everything. When the day of the competition came, she felt sure everything would fall into place. She would show everyone just how adventurous she could be, and they would no longer refer to her as "dull, boring, predictable Elizabeth."

"Look who just came in wearing the biggest grin I've ever seen," Todd said, nodding toward the door and munching on a fry.

Jessica stood at the doorway, surveying the Dairi Burger, with Lila at her side. She spotted some friends in the back and started heading toward them.

As Jessica approached Elizabeth's table, she stopped and said, "Liz, what are you doing here? Why aren't you spending the day working on your wonderful science project?" Jessica rolled her eyes at Lila.

"We were rained out," Elizabeth answered.

"What a shame," Jessica teased. "I hope you and Todd found something just as exciting to do."

"Actually, we played Scrabble," Todd answered, giving Jessica a wry smile.

Elizabeth turned a little red.

"I don't know how you can stand so much excitement, Liz," Lila remarked.

"And what have *you* done with your afternoon?"

"Nothing much," Jessica said coyly as she walked away. "We went shopping."

Todd and Elizabeth looked at each other and shook their heads, smiling. Elizabeth knew that Jessica was up to something, and it involved getting back at Caroline Pearce. But she wasn't sure exactly what Jessica had been doing in the name of revenge.

She and Todd had just about finished their french fries when Enid Rollins came up to the table.

"Enid, I didn't know you were here," Elizabeth said.

"It's so crowded that I didn't see you at first, either," Enid answered. "I have to tell you what I just overheard. Jessica and Lila were sitting at the table next to where I was sitting, and they were telling Amy all about what they did at the Unique Boutique today. Poor Caroline!"

"Sit down and tell me *everything!*" Elizabeth said, moving over to make room for Enid.

Elizabeth was putting the finishing touches on an English paper Saturday afternoon when the phone rang. She raced to pick it up, since she had a feeling Sean was going to call about their lesson. She didn't want anyone to start wondering who her new friend was.

"Hello?"

"Hi, Liz."

"Sean!" Elizabeth responded. "What a beautiful day."

"The rain looks like it's finished, anyway," Sean said.

"We couldn't ask for a better day to go surfing, could we?" exclaimed Elizabeth.

"Well, Liz," Sean began with a little hesitation in his voice, "I'm not so sure about that."

"What do you mean?" Elizabeth asked. "There's not a cloud in the sky."

"No, but the sea is still a little bit rough," Sean responded.

"You can't keep me from surfing another day!" Elizabeth exclaimed. "The competition is next week, and we only have a few more lessons."

"Listen, Liz," Sean said. "There are some pretty serious waves at Moon Beach today. Are you sure you can handle them?"

"I'm a strong swimmer."

"I don't know how great I feel about it, Liz," Sean answered.

"Sean," Elizabeth began in a confident voice, "I'm *certain* I can handle it. That is, as long as you're around."

"Well, I guess it'll be OK . . ." Sean said slowly.

"Great!" Elizabeth cried. "But I may be a little bit late. My sister needs the car today, so I'm going to have to take the bus."

"Oh, I'll pick you up," Sean suggested.

"I won't have you picking me up to drive me to a free lesson," Elizabeth said. *And I don't want to risk anyone seeing you here*, she added to herself.

"OK, if you say so. Well, hop on that bus and let's get to work!" Sean said cheerfully.

Eight

A little shiver ran down Elizabeth's spine as she watched the big waves crashing against the shore. She pulled a chunk of wax from her bag, knelt in the warm sand, and began to wax her board. "It looks pretty rough out there," she said nervously.

"It is," Sean said. "Before you got here, I went out for a few rides just to test the water. It was definitely exciting. Those waves *are* huge. But I'm going to leave it up to you, Liz. If you think you can handle it, then we'll have a lesson. If you don't think you can, then we won't."

"That makes sense, Sean," Elizabeth answered. "But to be perfectly honest, I really think I should give it a try. What if the water's like this on the day of the competition? Think of how much better I'll perform if I've done it before."

"You may be right, Liz," Sean said, "but I'll leave the decision up to you."

"Well, I didn't ride the bus all the way up

here just to *talk* about surfing!" Elizabeth exclaimed.

"I wouldn't mind if you did," Sean said, smiling.

"So, what should I work on today?" Elizabeth asked, quickly changing the subject.

"Today you should keep working on your pullout," Sean answered. "A well-executed pullout will win you lots of points with the judges."

Elizabeth put the wax in her bag and picked up the surfboard.

"Also, Liz," Sean added in a serious voice, "there are some riptides out there, so you should be extra careful."

"Right!" Elizabeth said confidently.

"And let me give you a little bit of advice. If you're about to wipe out in a really big wave, like the ones out there," Sean continued, nodding to the ocean, "take a big breath, and I mean *big*. And then if the wave tosses you around underwater, and you get disoriented, remember to head toward the light. The light means air and sky, and darkness means the bottom of the ocean. Got it?"

"Take a big breath and head toward the light," Elizabeth answered. She nodded confidently.

"Right," Sean said, gazing steadily into Elizabeth's eyes.

"Here goes nothing," Elizabeth said as she headed toward the crashing waves.

Once she got into the water, she discovered that the waves *were* stronger than she had expected. She had to admit, it was a little scary. As she paddled out, it seemed as if the waves *sounded* louder. Nobody else was surfing that day, and she felt lonely and isolated out there by herself.

Take a big breath and head for the light, she repeated to herself as she paddled.

She finally saw the wave she wanted. It was a big, swelling wave with a beautiful white top. Elizabeth turned her board toward the shore and then felt the swell of the wave lift her from behind. But it wasn't like anything she had ever felt before! The wave seemed to pick her up and toss her around like a piece of driftwood, and she struggled to stay in control. Finally, after a split second of desperate paddling, Elizabeth turned her board and felt it begin to slide along the wave. She was terrified, but somehow she found the strength to stand up.

As she rode the wave, she couldn't help but feel that something was wrong. Usually at this point in a ride, she felt in control. But right then she felt just the opposite.

She glanced over her shoulder and saw the huge wave beginning to crash down on top of her. She tried to brace herself for the impact, and then she took a deep breath.

The water crashed over her, and the surfboard slipped out from under her. Just as Elizabeth was rising to the surface to get another breath, she felt a powerful thud on the side of her head, and suddenly everything went blurry.

Elizabeth was sinking deeper into the wave when she felt a strong current catch hold of her. It dragged her down as if a great chain were attached to her legs, pulling her deeper and deeper into the water.

Elizabeth felt her heart constrict. *I'm caught in a riptide*, she suddenly realized.

Her body was crying out for air. Forgetting for a moment that she was underwater, she took a desperate breath. Then everything went black as night.

Elizabeth slowly blinked her eyes. Everything looked blurry and out of focus. She thought she felt something on her mouth and nose, but she couldn't figure out what it was.

Then suddenly her eyes cleared, and she saw Sean's face coming down to hers. She felt his mouth against hers, and then she felt her lungs expand with warm air. He was giving her mouth-to-mouth resuscitation.

When Sean saw Elizabeth's opened eyes, he immediately lifted his mouth from hers.

"Liz!" he cried, a look of utter relief on his handsome face. "Are you all right? I was so worried."

"Sean?" she managed. "What happened?"

"That doesn't matter now," Sean answered. "What matters is that you're alive."

In a flash, Elizabeth remembered the terror of being dragged deep into the wave. It was the most frightening experience she had ever had. If Sean hadn't been there, she probably would have died. And when she thought of that—and never seeing her family and friends again—she began to cry. Without thinking, Elizabeth reached up to Sean for comfort, and Sean immediately wrapped his arms tightly around her.

For a few minutes, Sean and Elizabeth embraced in the sand, and Elizabeth continued to cry. She held on tightly to Sean, as if she were still in danger of drowning, and Sean kept whispering, "It's all right, Liz, it's all right."

When Elizabeth felt safe again, she pulled away from Sean and wiped her eyes.

"How do you feel?" Sean asked.

"A little shaken up," Elizabeth said. "But thanks to you I'm going to be just fine."

"Let me check your eyes," Sean said, leaning close to Elizabeth's face. "When the board hit your head, you might have gotten a concussion, and I want to check your pupils."

Elizabeth opened and shut her eyes for Sean. He gazed into her eyes and then gave her nose a little kiss. "No concussion," he said.

"What happened out there, anyway?" Elizabeth asked, pulling away from Sean and wrapping a towel around her shoulders.

"When you wiped out, your board came down on your head," Sean began. "That probably disoriented you, and you couldn't figure out which way was up. Then the riptide got hold of you, and you must have taken a big breath of water. I saw all of this happen and jumped in after you. You were pretty far out, and I really had to swim fast. Finally I grabbed you and pulled you back to shore, then started giving you mouth-to-mouth."

"Sean, what can I . . . I mean, how can I ever thank you?"

"I was just doing my duty for my student," Sean said, smiling. And then he added, "I guess this means you'll probably want to pull out of the surfing competition."

"I don't give up *that* easily," Elizabeth replied. "My father always used to tell my sister and me, 'Whenever you fall off a horse, you've got to get right back on it, or you'll never get on it again.' So maybe at our next lesson I'll be ready to try again—that is, if the waves are smaller."

"So there's going to be a next lesson?" Sean asked, his face brightening.

"Of course," Elizabeth said.

As the two of them walked back slowly to the clubhouse, Sean put his arm gently around Elizabeth's shoulders. She knew she should tell him not to, but for some reason she couldn't bring herself to say it.

As they walked on across the sand, Elizabeth couldn't help but think that their hug on the beach had changed things between them. She hoped, more than anything else, that she hadn't led Sean on by holding him so tightly. But her instinct told her that Sean thought the hug meant much more than it did.

Sean carried Elizabeth's surfboard to the clubhouse and put it on its stand. When he came back outside, there was a gentle glimmer in his green eyes.

"Liz," he began, "would you like to go out for some dinner tonight?"

"I'd love to, Sean," Elizabeth answered, "but I'm having dinner with Todd tonight."

She was relieved to have such a good excuse. And she couldn't wait to see Todd. After this frightening day, it would be nice to curl up safely in his arms.

"Too bad," Sean said sadly.

Elizabeth looked down at her watch, and her heart skipped a beat. Todd would be showing up at her door in exactly half an hour!

"Well, if I can't have dinner with you," Sean began, "can I at least drive you home? After a day like this, you shouldn't have to deal with the bus."

"Now, that's an offer I can't refuse," she said, hurrying Sean out to his Jeep. They buckled up, and Sean pulled the Jeep out into traffic. Elizabeth tapped her fingers nervously against her leg as he drove. She hoped they would get home before Todd showed up.

Thirty minutes later they turned onto the Wakefields' street. Elizabeth's heart sank when she saw Todd's car in her driveway.

"Stop right here!" she cried.

"Here?" asked Sean, confused. He pulled his car in front of an ultramodern home two houses down from the Wakefields'. "But you told me you lived in a split-level house."

"Did I say that?" Elizabeth replied, her face turning red. "Maybe I meant our other house, the little vacation place we have up in the mountains."

"I didn't know you had a vacation house," Sean said.

I didn't know we had one, either! Elizabeth thought. "We don't use it much," she replied. Then she nervously cleared her throat. "Well, Sean," she said, "I can't thank you enough for what you did today."

"I'm glad I was there to help," Sean said modestly, smiling at her.

"I'll see you on Tuesday at the clubhouse," Elizabeth said, stepping out of the car.

"Great!" Sean cried, waving as he drove away. Elizabeth waved back and slowly made her way up her neighbor's walkway. As soon as Sean's car disappeared, she turned and hurried down the sidewalk toward her house.

Todd was waiting for her in the hallway, with his arms crossed. Elizabeth was still pretty shaken up after the accident, and even just the sight of Todd's familiar dark brown eyes and tall, lean figure made her want to fall into his arms and feel safe again.

"Hi, Todd," she said, giving him a kiss on the cheek.

"Hello, Elizabeth," Todd responded coolly.

"Sorry I'm late, but things got busy up at Moon Beach," Elizabeth said, blushing a little.

"I'm just here to tell you that I have an extra-credit project I have to work on tonight, so I can't take you to dinner," Todd said flatly.

"You're doing schoolwork on a Saturday night?" Elizabeth cried.

"It came up suddenly. So maybe I'll see you in school on Monday or something." Todd turned and opened the front door.

"Todd, wait!" Elizabeth cried, reaching out for his arm.

"I'll see you later, Liz," Todd said, and then he slammed the door behind him.

Elizabeth stared at the door for a moment, stunned. And then she burst into tears and ran up the stairs to her room.

She shut the door behind her and buried her face in her pillow. She knew that Todd had seen Sean's car! And then he'd made up the story about some extra-credit project just to get out of dinner.

Everything seemed to be going wrong. Not only had she almost drowned, but she had probably led Sean on by hugging him that afternoon. And now Todd had just broken their date—and slammed the door in her face!

I wish I'd never tried to change at all! Elizabeth thought as she wiped her tears away with a tissue. *It's just not worth it!*

Nine

On Monday Elizabeth and Todd were eating lunch together in the cafeteria.

"I called you a couple of times yesterday, but you weren't home," Elizabeth said quietly.

"I was playing ball with the guys," Todd replied. He took a bite of his sandwich.

"Oh," Elizabeth answered quietly. "I see." She took a deep breath and then let out a big sigh.

"You know, Todd," she said at last, "I was really sad that we didn't go out to dinner Saturday night. I was looking forward to seeing you so much."

"Yeah, well, schoolwork comes first," Todd said, shrugging. "But I guess you know all about *that*."

"I know things have been a little weird lately," Elizabeth remarked. "But everything will be better once I've given my big presentation."

"We just haven't been seeing enough of each other," Todd commented sadly.

"I know," Elizabeth said.

"So I was thinking, maybe we could go to the baseball game on Thursday," Todd said.

"Oh, Todd," Elizabeth said with a frustrated sigh. "I really can't! Thursday is the last day to work on my project before the presentation on Saturday."

"I should have known," Todd replied, tapping his spoon against his milk carton.

"I'm really sorry," Elizabeth said. "But it will all be over soon."

Todd hesitated for a moment and then said, "If I didn't know you better, Liz, I'd almost guess you were seeing another guy."

Elizabeth's heart seemed to stop. "Why do you say that?" she asked. "I'd never do that to you."

"Then who was that guy who dropped you off down the street on Saturday, when I came to pick you up for dinner?" Todd asked.

"Oh, him!" Elizabeth said, laughing nervously. "He's one of my research partners."

"Then why did you have him stop at the other end of the street?" Todd asked, fiddling with his straw. "And why did you go up the neighbor's walk?"

What have I gotten myself into, Elizabeth wondered. "Listen, Todd !" Elizabeth said desperately. "I know things may seem a little weird right now. But I just *know* everything will be better after the presentation!"

"Let me tell you," he said, crossing his arms, a sullen took on his face, "this better be one special presentation."

"I think it will be," she said. "At least I *hope* it will be."

Todd looked searchingly at Elizabeth, then shook his head. "I hope it will be, too," he said, rising to his feet. "I've got to finish up a few problems before math, so I guess I'll see you later."

Elizabeth said goodbye and watched Todd saunter out of the cafeteria. She hated hurting Todd more than anything in the world. But after keeping her real project a secret for so long, she didn't want to ruin the surprise now. She only hoped that making him wait wouldn't end up ruining their relationship.

Just then, she saw Jessica approaching with Lila and Amy at her side.

"Hey, Liz," Jessica said, sitting down. "What's new with you?"

Elizabeth shrugged. "Not much."

"I hardly see you anymore, what with that project of yours," Jessica said.

"Did you find a way to get seaweed off the beaches yet?" Lila asked. "I hate swimming with that stuff—it's so slimy and gross."

"No, that's not exactly what I'm working on," Elizabeth said, laughing.

"Well, I'm sure it's just fascinating, whatever it is," Amy said, rolling her eyes.

"You'll see," Elizabeth promised. "Actually, Jess, I'm glad you came over here. I've been meaning to talk to you about something."

"Uh-oh," Jessica said. "Sounds like I'm in trouble."

"I heard about what you've been doing to Caroline at the Unique Boutique," Elizabeth said. "And I think it's terrible."

The three girls started giggling.

"I mean it, Jess," Elizabeth continued. She looked at the other girls. "I think you *all* should give her a break."

"But Caroline made the mistake of crossing Jessica Wakefield," Amy commented and laughed.

"I've seen you do stuff like this dozens of times before, Jess," Elizabeth said. "And you always end up getting in trouble."

"That's a chance I'm willing to take," Jessica answered. "Besides, I've got Caroline right where I want her."

"You sure do," Lila and Amy chimed at once.

"So let *me* worry about Caroline," Jessica added, lifting her eyebrows playfully. "And you just worry about your project!"

Smiling, Elizabeth watched the three girls rush out of the cafeteria.

Turtle eggs and seaweed? she thought, standing up. *Do they ever have a surprise coming to them!*

* * *

"Liz, listen to me," Sean began, following Elizabeth across the sand the next day. "Are you sure you want to surf today? I mean, you don't have to prove anything to me."

"I know that," Elizabeth replied firmly, dropping her board in the sand and kneeling down to wax it. "But maybe I have to prove something to *myself*."

"You know, Liz," Sean began, "I don't care about that competition. The only thing I care about is you and your safety."

"That's very sweet of you, Sean," Elizabeth replied, applying the last touches of wax to her bright purple board. "But I think I'd like to surf, anyway."

Elizabeth was putting on a very brave front, but she was trembling inside. In fact, she couldn't remember a time when she had been so nervous. She could hardly believe she was about to get back into the water—just three days after she had nearly drowned.

Her stomach was twisting and turning, and the palms of her hands were sweaty. She even shivered with cold a few times, even though the bright mid-afternoon sun was shining right on her.

"Just be careful," Sean said, looking deep into her eyes. "I don't know what I'd do if anything happened to you."

Elizabeth didn't like it when Sean acted so

serious about her, but the look in his eyes was so genuine and sweet that Elizabeth couldn't bring herself to tell him to back off.

"Look at the ocean, Sean," Elizabeth said. "It's a perfect day for surfing."

There was no doubt about that. The sky was clear, the sun was warm, and the sea looked calm and steady. There were lots of kids from Big Mesa hanging out and talking on the beach, and quite a few surfers were out taking advantage of the beautiful day and better-than-average waves.

Just then Laurie MacNeil came strolling down from the clubhouse, wearing a skimpy bikini.

"Hi, Liz," she said. "I heard about your accident, and I just wanted to say how glad I am that you're OK."

"Thanks, Laurie," Elizabeth said.

"And you're so brave to get right back out there," Laurie continued. "But I guess I'd feel safe, too, with Sean watching me."

"He *is* a great teacher." Elizabeth gave Sean a smile.

"You guys are making me blush," Sean said. "But don't let that stop you!"

"Hey, Laurie, did I see you surfing a couple of weeks ago?" Elizabeth asked. "It was pretty late in the afternoon, but I could have sworn it was you."

"Are you kidding?" Sean interrupted. "When

I see Laurie surfing, then I'll know something strange is up." He laughed good-naturedly.

"What do you mean?" Laurie asked, setting her hands playfully on her hips.

"You've just never shown an ounce of interest in doing any surfing, that's all," Sean answered.

"Well, I guess I saw someone who just looked like you," Elizabeth said to Laurie.

"It must have been someone else," Laurie said as she turned to walk away. "Good luck in the surfing competition, Liz."

"Thanks. Will you be watching?" Elizabeth asked.

"Definitely," Laurie replied. "See you guys later!" She ran off to join some friends on the beach.

"Laurie is really nice," Elizabeth commented after the girl had disappeared. "And she's so pretty."

"She *did* look kind of good," Sean admitted.

"I guess not everybody wants to be as daring and adventurous as we are!" Elizabeth said as she marched into the water with her surfboard under her arm.

"Hey, remember to stay to the back of the board and crouch down low when you're pulling out," Sean called out. "That's what the judges look for."

"All right!" Elizabeth cried.

But her confidence started to fade as she waded deeper into the water. And her stomach started churning even more as she began to paddle out across the powerful waves. She could feel her heart thumping in her chest.

But she *did* have a point to prove to herself. She had started this whole surfing thing to be more daring and unpredictable. And this was going to be the ultimate test.

Elizabeth caught sight of the perfect wave. It swelled up gently—it was powerful, but not too wild. She turned her board toward the shore and waited to feel the lift of the wave. She tried to stay calm, so she wouldn't make some big mistake and end up wiping out.

She felt the wave lift her board, and then she turned the board to the left and felt it dip down. The surfboard began to slide along the wave, but as hard as Elizabeth tried, she couldn't stand up. Her legs were literally paralyzed with fear. In fact, nothing at all seemed to work! She was telling her legs and arms to move, but they were ignoring her. What if she crashed into the water and was still unable to move?

But then, a second later, like magic, she rose to her feet. The surfboard was gliding along perfectly. All of her confidence rushed back in a giant wave. She even let out a loud "Yahoo!" as she sped along. She had done it!

Elizabeth rode the wave perfectly. When the

wave began to break on shore, she leaned back on the board, crouched down, and neatly pulled out of the wave. Sean was clapping and whistling wildly on the beach; then he waved his arms and smiled.

When Elizabeth walked out of the ocean, Sean ran over and gave her a big hug. "Well," he said proudly, "there's no doubt now that you're ready for the competition!"

"You know what?" Elizabeth responded, feeling exhilarated. "I think you're right!"

"You did a great job today, Liz. Maybe we should celebrate your comeback," Sean said. "Let's go to the beach café, and I'll buy you anything you want."

Sean and Elizabeth had just gotten to the clubhouse that afternoon, after an hour and a half of hard practice.

"That's very nice of you, Sean," she began, "but I really have other things I should do."

"Oh," Sean responded glumly.

Why does he have to look so brokenhearted? Elizabeth thought. "Well . . . maybe one soda wouldn't hurt," she said and grinned at him.

"Great!" Sean exclaimed, his face brightening immediately. He turned around and called, "Hey, Sammy? Would you mind closing up for me tonight? Something's just come up."

"Sure thing," Sammy said and gave Sean a wink, which made Elizabeth uncomfortable.

Without another word, Sean led Elizabeth across the sand to the Moon Beach Café. He ordered a hamburger, fries, and a malt, and Elizabeth ordered a soda. They sat down outside under a yellow umbrella.

"I want to propose a toast," Sean began, lifting his vanilla malt. "To a very brave surfer—and a beautiful girl."

Elizabeth blushed. "Thanks, Sean," she mumbled. And then—just to change the subject as quickly as possible—she added, "You know, I've been thinking of doing an article on surfing for our school newspaper."

"Oh, really?" Sean said.

Elizabeth nodded. "I thought I could write about everything you've taught me. I think everyone who doesn't surf would be interested in the different moves in surfing and the equipment, like your Simmons board, and the fact that it's worth so much money."

"That sounds like a great idea!" Sean exclaimed. "And that reminds me—I have an offer to make to you."

"Oh, really . . ." Elizabeth said hesitantly.

"Yeah. I'd like you to use my Simmons in the competition."

"Sean!" Elizabeth gasped. "I couldn't. It's your prize possession!"

"I've thought about it, and you're the only one I would ever let use it," Sean answered. He reached across the table and took Elizabeth's hand. "In these last couple of days, I really feel like something's been happening between us."

"But the board's worth thousands of dollars," Elizabeth protested, pulling her hand away. "And what if I lose it or break it—or even so much as *scratch* it?"

"Then it'll have been scratched for a good cause," Sean said. "So that's the end of the discussion. It's one of the best boards ever made, and I want you to use it!"

She felt strange about agreeing, especially after Sean had taken her hand. But she just couldn't bring herself to say no to him. He seemed so eager for her to do well in the competition, and she knew it wasn't just because of the bet.

The truth was, Elizabeth couldn't quite figure out how to deal with Sean's feelings for her. He knew she had a boyfriend, but that didn't seem to make much of a difference to him. Was he ever going to give up? she wondered.

Ten

"I guess I *have* to go, since you're my sister," Jessica said, rolling her eyes. "But I can think of about a million more interesting things to do on a Saturday afternoon."

It was Wednesday, and Elizabeth was walking through the cafeteria, inviting people to her presentation at the Moon Beach Marine Biology Center.

"And, Lila and Amy, you guys are invited, too," Elizabeth added. "I know it sounds kind of dull, but I think you might end up being surprised."

"I'll have to check my schedule," Lila said, lifting her nose. "I may have something planned for Saturday afternoon."

"I may have something planned, too," Amy added, clearing her throat.

"Oh, no, you don't," Jessica remarked, shaking her finger at her friends. "If *I* have to go to some boring presentation, then you guys have to come along, too!"

"But we've been helping you with *everything* these days," Lila said, pouting. "And look at the thanks we get. Without us, you would have been kicked out of the Unique Boutique long ago."

"Speaking of the Unique Boutique, Jess," Elizabeth began, "I really hope you're not planning to go back—"

"Stop right there, Liz," Jessica interrupted, holding up her hand. "I'm going to suffer enough with this marine biology thing—I don't need a lecture, too!"

"OK, OK," Elizabeth said with a laugh. She stole a potato chip from Jessica's bag and then turned to walk away.

She found Todd sitting with Winston Egbert at a table in the corner.

"Hi, Todd. Hi, Win," she said, swinging down into the chair beside him. "I just wanted to remind you guys that you're both invited to my marine biology presentation on Saturday."

"Can't wait," Winston said. "I'll be sure to bring a pillow and an alarm clock."

"I should be able to make it," Todd said distantly. "Unless something comes up."

"Oh, Todd," Elizabeth cried, "you *have* to be there! It won't be any fun at all without you."

"Fun?" Todd said glumly. "We haven't had any *fun* together for weeks."

"Please, Todd!" Elizabeth pleaded. "Promise me you'll be there."

As Todd stood up to leave, he gave Elizabeth a searching glance. "OK, I'll be there," he said. Then he turned and left the cafeteria.

Elizabeth continued making the rounds, inviting people to Moon Beach, but she was afraid she would start crying at any minute. Todd had never seemed so distant. She had a feeling she was losing Todd, and all because of a stupid dare she had given *herself*! No one had made her do it, after all.

Finally she spotted Enid, and her heart lifted a little. At least she had her best friend to talk to! *In fact,* Elizabeth thought as she hurried over to Enid's table, *I feel like telling Enid everything. I've got to get all this off my chest—even if it does ruin the surprise.*

"Enid, I'm so happy to see you," Elizabeth said, dropping into a chair beside her friend.

"Liz, what's wrong?" Enid asked. "You look upset."

"Enid, it seems like everything's going wrong lately," Elizabeth said. "And mostly it has to do with this big project that I've been keeping secret from everybody."

"Oh, the marine biology thing," Enid said with a little yawn. Even she seemed to think that a marine biology project was a bore.

"Yes. The marine biology thing—or what I've been *calling* the marine biology thing."

Enid regarded her friend. "What do you mean? Aren't you actually doing a special project?"

Elizabeth hesitated.

"Didn't you invite me up to the Moon Beach Marine Biology Center on Saturday, to watch some kind of big presentation?" Enid asked.

"Of course," Elizabeth exclaimed, taking a deep breath to collect herself. "But it's more complicated than that. You see, I've been sick and tired of everybody thinking I'm boring and unadventurous. So a little while ago I decided to do something different, and I—"

"Hey, guys" Caroline Pearce said. She sat down at the table. "What's new?"

"Oh, not much, I guess," Elizabeth said wearily. She could tell by the glimmer in Caroline's eyes that she had something juicy to tell them.

"Well, work at the Unique Boutique is going really well for me," Caroline gushed, to Elizabeth's surprise. "Of course, my boss is a real nightmare. She's constantly telling me, 'The customer always comes first.' Can you believe it? I mean, most of the customers we get in there should come *last*, in my opinion."

Elizabeth knew Caroline was referring to Jessica, but she decided to keep silent.

"I haven't been to see the store yet," Enid said innocently.

"Oh, then you'd better hurry up," Caroline answered. She cleared her throat and added, "I mean, you'd better hurry up because a lot of really cute outfits are going to be taken off the racks soon, to make room for next season's clothes. But everything in the store is just fabulous."

"It sounds as though you really like working there, Caroline," Enid remarked.

"It's not a bad place to work," Caroline replied. "But there is one *really* interesting thing. There's a new salesgirl starting work next week who bears a really weird resemblance to someone we all once knew. And I'll bet someone in the Wakefield family would be *very* interested to see her."

"What are you talking about, Caroline?" Elizabeth asked.

"Oh, sorry, guys!" Caroline exclaimed, rising from her chair and checking her watch. "Gotta run! See you soon!"

"But, Caroline—" Enid protested as Caroline hurried out of the cafeteria.

"What do you think *that* was all about?" she said, turning to Elizabeth.

"Who knows! I'm not going to worry about it, though."

"You're probably right, Liz," Enid said as the bell rang. Both girls stood up and headed out to the busy corridor. "But tell me what you were going to say earlier, about being boring and all that."

"Oh, that," Elizabeth answered with a wave of her hand. "Nothing important. Just promise me you'll be at my presentation on Saturday."

110

"I wouldn't miss it!" Enid answered with a smile.

The next time Jessica decided to terrorize the Unique Boutique happened to be that very afternoon, even though neither Amy nor Lila would come along.

As soon as Jessica opened the door, Caroline Pearce rushed over to her with a sweet smile.

"Hello, Jessica," she said politely. "How may I help you this afternoon?"

Jessica had to admit she was a little confused by this sudden burst of good manners. What had happened to the old Caroline, who tried to avoid waiting on Jessica as if she had the plague? But Jessica wasn't going to be fooled by whatever Caroline was up to. She would proceed with her scheme exactly as planned.

"Oh, hello, Caroline," Jessica answered. "I thought I might like to try on a few things this afternoon."

"Please, help yourself!" Caroline smiled again. "In fact, we just got a whole new batch of cute sweaters that I know you'll like. Follow me. I just stacked them over here," she said helpfully.

Jessica followed Caroline through the crowded store to a tall, neat stack of sweaters. Then Jessica began pulling sweaters out from the bottoms of stacks and tossing the ones she didn't want in messy heaps on the counters. She did the same with the pants, until she had an armful of clothes to try on.

But all Caroline did was follow her and sweetly suggest other things Jessica might like to take into the dressing room.

"You know what, Jessica?" Caroline said. "I don't think you've ever tried on any of our shoes, have you?"

"No, as a matter of fact, I haven't," Jessica responded.

"Let me find you some flats that I think would look great with that plaid skirt you're trying on," Caroline offered. She disappeared for a minute and returned with three shoe boxes.

She handed them to Jessica, who by now was so weighted down with clothes that she could barely carry the shoes.

"Here, let me help you carry some of that," Caroline offered, taking half of the stuff Jessica was holding. "And let me find you an empty changing room."

Jessica looked around to see if the manager was watching. Maybe that was the reason Caroline was acting so strange. But the manager was busy with another customer at the opposite end of the store.

"Here's a changing room, Jess," Caroline said, opening the door and setting the heap of clothes on the small wooden bench inside.

Jessica followed her and added her own load of clothes to the pile.

"Take your time to work through that," Caroline said, smiling sweetly. "In the meantime, I'll go out and look around the store for more cute things in your size. OK?"

"Sure," Jessica replied, returning Caroline's overly sweet smile.

What in the world is she up to? Jessica wondered as she began to try things on. After taking off each item, she tossed it haphazardly onto the floor, making a large pile.

Just when Jessica had taken off a skirt and blouse and was standing there wearing next to nothing, Caroline opened the door to the changing room and began to pick up the clothes scattered everywhere.

"I'll take some things back for you so there's room in here for all the other stuff I've found." Caroline scooped up all the clothes and shoes in big armfuls. Jessica stood and watched.

"I'll be right back," Caroline said, closing the door behind her.

Suddenly something occurred to Jessica, and she looked around the room in panic. There wasn't a single stitch of clothing left anywhere.

"Hey, Caroline!" she called out. "You took *my* clothes away, too!"

But there was no response. Jessica stood in the empty changing room in her underwear, turning red with anger. *Caroline's boss is going to hear about this*, she thought. *And then Caroline will really be in trouble!*

Just then, she heard Caroline's voice ring out from somewhere in the store. "No, I *won't* put away that huge stack of clothes!" Caroline yelled.

"If you want to keep your job, you will," threatened another voice, which Jessica immediately recognized as that of Caroline's manager.

"As of this paycheck, I've earned all the money I need!" Caroline exclaimed. "So I don't need you or this lousy job for one more second. I've had just about enough of being pushed around by you and your rude customers! I *quit!*"

"You can't quit because you're *fired!*" the manager screamed.

Jessica opened the door of the changing room just a crack and saw Caroline marching toward her with her clothes in her arms.

"Hey, Caroline, give me my clothes back!" Jessica hissed.

"Oh, thanks for stopping by, Magenta," Caroline purred and gave Jessica a sly, triumphant smile. "Bye, now," she said with a little wave as she passed by the changing room and walked out into the Sweet Valley Mall, carrying all of Jessica's clothes.

The next day Jessica was sitting with Lila and

Amy, eating lunch and trying to hide her face. She was so humiliated! It wasn't even noon yet, and the whole school seemed to know what had happened at the Unique Boutique the day before.

Winston Egbert walked up to Elizabeth, who was at the next table over with Enid.

"Now, Liz," Winston began in a loud voice so that Jessica could hear him, "I know you're the responsible, sensible twin, so please don't let Jessica go shopping by herself ever again!"

"Why do you say that, Winston?" Elizabeth asked, giving her twin a knowing glance.

"Because Jess could end up losing all her clothes again," Winston said, "and she might get arrested for indecent exposure this time."

Enid, Lila, Amy, and Elizabeth erupted into laughter, but Jessica scowled.

"C'mon, Jess," Elizabeth said with a smile. "You've got to admit, Caroline did a pretty good job on you."

"I don't have to admit *anything*," she said. Crossing her arms, she glared at her twin.

Everybody laughed again, and Jessica felt her face turn red.

"You know, Liz," Jessica said, "I don't know if I can face going to your biology presentation on Saturday. It'll be too humiliating."

"But, Jess—" Elizabeth began to protest.

"You're just looking for an excuse to get out of *learning* something," Enid broke in.

"Hey, I have some news that might interest you, Jess," Lila said. "There happens to be a big surfing competition on Moon Beach, right before Liz's presentation. I was thinking of going to that anyway. You can just sneak over to the Marine Biology Center for a few minutes."

"A surfing competition?" Jessica answered, suddenly becoming more interested. *Think of all the cute guys who will be there.* And none of them would have heard anything about her humiliation at the Unique Boutique. This was an opportunity she couldn't pass up.

"Well, maybe I *will* show up at your presentation, after all," Jessica said. "Even though I'm sure it won't be as interesting as the surfing competition."

"That's perfect," Elizabeth said. "Why don't you all go to the surfing competition, and then when it's over, you can just walk over to the Moon Beach Marine Biology Center."

"If we can find it," Amy said, winking at Lila.

"Hang ten?" Sean cried, looking at Elizabeth in disbelief. "Do you have any idea how hard it is to hang ten? You've got to have perfect board control."

"Don't you think I'm ready yet, Sean?" asked Elizabeth, waxing her board on the beach.

"Well . . ." Sean began, giving the matter some thought. "The fact is, you're already a pretty good surfer. And since this is our last official lesson . . ."

"Great!" Elizabeth cried, picking up her surfboard. "And even if I wipe out, it'll still be fun to *try*."

"OK, Liz," Sean began, shaking his head. "If you can hang ten on your first try, then I guarantee that you have the talent to win the competition on Saturday."

"I won't be able to do anything until you tell me what to do," Elizabeth said, impatient to get the lesson under way.

"OK, Liz," Sean began, "the hardest part about hanging ten is walking to the tip of the surfboard. You have to do it quickly and keep your weight on the back foot. Then you've got to curl all your toes over the end of the board: that's hanging ten. And, believe me, it's a whole lot harder than it sounds."

A few minutes later, after she was standing and sliding along a wave, Elizabeth took her first steps toward the end of the board. The whole time she kept expecting herself to go plunging into the surf and wipe out . . . but the next thing she knew, she was crouched down

117

at the very front of her surfboard. And then she inched up a little bit more and felt her toes hang off the sides of the board! She rode the wave, hanging ten, for fifteen glorious seconds before the wave broke on top of her and she wiped out.

Elizabeth emerged from the water with a triumphant smile on her face.

Sean was standing in the sand, clapping and cheering, along with Sammy and Dave, who had gathered around to watch.

"That was awesome!" Dave exclaimed.

Elizabeth smiled. "All the credit goes to my teacher," she said, nodding to Sean.

"No, no," Sean said, literally beaming with pride. "Elizabeth would have been a great surfer even without me."

"With talent like that," Sammy added, "this girl's a cinch to win the competition."

"Or at least she'll give the rest of the girls a run for their money," Dave said.

"Hey, Sean," Sammy said, "looks like your bet is a sure thing. What kind of surfboard are you going to make us buy for you?"

"Another Simmons?" Dave suggested teasingly.

"No, not an original Simmons," Sean said, laughing. "But I *have* offered Liz the use of *my* Simmons in the competition."

"Oooh, then she *is* a special girl," S‑nmy teased, nudging Sean with his elbow.

"Yeah, you must really like her," Dave added, "if you're going to lend her your prize board.

Abruptly Elizabeth picked up her rental board and headed toward the clubhouse. She didn't like being referred to as Sean's "special girl."

"Hey, Liz," Sean said, running to catch up with her. "You did a *great* job out there. I can't believe you actually were able to hang ten."

"It was fun," Elizabeth replied quietly.

"I want you to relax and get plenty of rest tomorrow, then I'll meet you here Saturday a half hour before the competition starts—for some last-minute coaching," Sean said.

Elizabeth could hardly believe her big moment was only two days away. *Imagine the looks on their faces when I show them I can hang ten!* she thought.

"OK, Sean, see you Saturday!" she said cheerfully. "I'll be ready for the waves."

"With that attitude, you'll definitely win!" Sean exclaimed.

Elizabeth crossed her fingers as she walked to her car. *I sure hope so.*

Eleven

By the time Elizabeth got to the clubhouse on Saturday, the beach was crowded with spectators. Tanned surfers were kneeling in the sand, carefully waxing their boards. There were bleachers set up in the sand, with long, colorful banners flying in the breeze. The day was perfect, with a clear sky and big—but not *too* big—waves.

Elizabeth was so excited that she could barely stand it. After the compliments she had been given at her last lesson, she was feeling too confident to be nervous. But she was excited that all of her friends would be here to watch her triumph. She imagined the looks on Todd's and Jessica's faces when her name was announced and she came walking out of the clubhouse with the surfboard under her arm.

Today she felt so strong that it would take a tidal wave to knock her off her board!

"Hey, Liz—over here!" Sean cried from the middle of the crowd. He walked toward Elizabeth, carrying his shining surfboard under his arm. "Well," he said, beaming as he handed Elizabeth the board, "here it is, my Simmons original."

"It's even more beautiful than I remembered," Elizabeth said.

"And here's the special wax I use," he said, handing her a small jar. "Now I have to help organize things here, so I'll be pretty busy. When you're out there, just remember everything I've taught you and you'll be fine. You can let the surfboard do the rest. Good luck, Liz!" He gave Elizabeth a little hug and a kiss on the cheek.

Elizabeth hugged him back and then set out to find a spot on the crowded beach to wax the surfboard. As soon as she found a place and was kneeling in the sand, she overheard a voice, one she recognized as Laurie MacNeil's.

"I really hope Sean notices me today," Laurie was saying to a friend. "I don't know why, but I feel like this is my last chance as far as he's concerned."

"I know how much you care about Sean," Laurie's friend replied. "I hope everything works out between you."

"I only hope I'm not fooling myself," Laurie continued, sighing. "Elizabeth Wakefield's a *fabulous* surfer. I don't think I've got much of a chance of standing out next to her."

"But you've been practicing every bit as hard as she has," her friend replied. "If not harder."

"But Sammy told me that Sean is lending Elizabeth his favorite surfboard for the competition," Laurie said sadly. "I know how much that board means to him. When I heard *that*, I almost gave up on Sean altogether."

"Don't talk like that!" her friend replied. "Just get out there and think about Sean and have the best ride of your life."

Elizabeth couldn't believe how dumb she'd been. She should have figured it out when Laurie tried to imply that she and Sean were a couple. Laurie MacNeil was in love with Sean! And she had obviously learned to surf just to impress him— and to win him away from Elizabeth.

If only there was some way to get Sean and Laurie together, Elizabeth thought. *Then, not only would they be happy, but I wouldn't have to worry anymore about hurting Sean's feelings or leading him on.*

It was the perfect solution. The problem was, how could she get Sean and Laurie together?

Just then, a plan popped into Elizabeth's mind. Her face brightened, and she picked up Sean's Simmons surfboard and ran across the crowded beach.

"Liz!" Sean cried, spinning around and gazing at her in surprise. "You're up in a few minutes. What are you doing here?"

"I've been trying to find you for fifteen minutes," Elizabeth exclaimed, out of breath, "but this crowd is so big."

"What's the matter?" Sean asked. "And hurry up—or you'll miss your turn."

"Sean," Elizabeth began, I can't use your surfboard. I mean, I've never surfed on it before, and this is a big competition. I think I'd be much better off using my old purple surfboard. I'm used to it."

"But I promise you that the Simmons will feel a thousand times better than your old purple thing," Sean said. "You'll have the best ride of your life on it."

"You may be right, Sean," Elizabeth answered firmly, "but I really don't think I should use it."

"But I don't understand," Sean said, looking hurt. "You know how much this means to me."

"Yes, I know, Sean," Elizabeth continued. "And maybe that's part of the reason why I *can't* use it."

"But I don't understand," Sean repeated.

"Maybe you will in a little while, Sean," Elizabeth responded, taking Sean's hand and giving it a firm shake. "And thanks for everything. You've been a great teacher!"

As Elizabeth hurried along the bleachers, she looked up and caught sight of the Sweet Valley crowd, cheering and clapping for the surfers. She could see Jessica and Amy and Lila. Near them she could see Enid. Even Winston was there with a bunch of his friends. But where was Todd?

All the excitement she had felt earlier seemed to vanish into thin air. *If Todd doesn't show up,* she thought, *then I have the terrible feeling it's over between us. And all for what? Just so I could prove to everyone I could take risks?*

Just then she saw Todd sit down beside Enid, with two cups of soda in his hands. Elizabeth laughed out loud and let out a big sigh of relief as she raced toward the clubhouse for the beat-up purple board.

Suddenly the announcer's voice came booming over the loudspeaker: "AND OUR NEXT COMPETITIOR IS . . . ELIZABETH WAKE-FIELD!"

"Elizabeth Wakefield?" Jessica nearly screamed.

"Did I just hear what I thought I heard?" Todd exclaimed.

Everybody from Sweet Valley was amazed.

"There must be some mistake," Todd said. "Liz doesn't know the first thing about surfing."

"I'm *sure* that Liz is up at the Marine Biology Center," Enid replied.

"This can't be my sister!" Jessica exclaimed. "Can you imagine Elizabeth surfing? No way!"

"There *must* be another Elizabeth Wakefield in Southern California," Lila said. "And besides, how could your sister rush from a surfing competition to her marine biology presentation?"

Just then, Elizabeth strode down the beach into the water, carrying a purple surfboard with a pink stripe down the middle. There was no doubting it now, Elizabeth was the next surfer. And a few moments later, after the shock wore off a little bit, the whole Sweet Valley section began to cheer for their friend.

"Go, Liz! Go, Liz! Go, Liz!" they cried, with Todd's and Jessica's voices the loudest of them all.

Even as she paddled out into the surf, Elizabeth could hear the cheering.

She really wanted to show everyone what kind of surfer she had become. She even wanted to show them that she could hang ten. Then they would know for sure that she could be as adventurous as anyone.

On the other hand, Elizabeth knew exactly what she had to do to get Sean and Laurie together.

But then she heard her friends yelling, "Go, Liz! Go, Liz! Go, Liz!"

Think of how amazed everyone would be if I won the competition, she thought. *Jessica wouldn't be able to make fun of me anymore. And think how proud Todd would be.*

Elizabeth felt she could win the competition. Her last few lessons had been terrific, and she had amazed even herself by hanging ten. *If I really wanted to,* Elizabeth thought to herself as she paddled out, *I could ride one of these waves forever!*

Just then, she caught sight of the perfect wave, rolling toward her. With her heart racing in her chest, Elizabeth turned her board toward the shore and felt the swell lift it up. The ride was going perfectly. Everything felt just right.

She paddled a few times, and the board turned effortlessly to the left, dropped down, and began to slide along the wave. Elizabeth thrilled to the feel of the ocean and her control over its great power. She rose quickly to her feet and rode the wave expertly for a few seconds.

But she knew what she had to do.

As everyone watched, Elizabeth seemed to lose her balance. The wave began to crest over her, and she hopped back on one foot like a clumsy beginner.

"It looks like she's going to wipe out!" Jessica gasped.

The board flipped out from under Elizabeth, and she went sprawling into the surf, her arms and legs flailing behind her. She landed with a giant belly flop.

"Oh, no!" Jessica cried, giggling. "That was too funny! Liz a surfer."

"She should stick to writing," Lila said.

"And museums," added Amy.

Todd shook his head and laughed. "So *this* is Elizabeth's presentation," he said to Enid with a grin. "What a surprise! No wonder she wanted to keep it a secret."

"Who would have thought that Liz would have the guts to enter a surfing competition?" Enid said proudly.

"And to think I was mad about it," Todd said, shaking his head and smiling. "She really had me fooled!"

Twelve

"NEXT IS LAURIE MACNEIL OF BIG MESA!" cried the announcer, just as Elizabeth was climbing out of the water.

Elizabeth saw Laurie making her way toward the ocean and made sure that Laurie noticed the old, beat-up purple board that she had used. Elizabeth wanted to be absolutely positive that Laurie knew she hadn't used Sean's special surfboard.

"Good luck, Laurie," Elizabeth cried as the two girls passed each other. "I hope you do better than I did!"

"Thanks," Laurie replied confidently.

Elizabeth stood for a minute, watching Laurie paddle out. Just then, Sean walked up and grabbed Elizabeth's arm.

"Liz, what happened out there?" he asked, his expression showing his disappointment.

"I don't know." Elizabeth shrugged. "Did you

hear? Laurie's the next competitor! Isn't that great?"

"Laurie *MacNeil*?" Sean asked.

Elizabeth nodded and pointed out at the water.

"What's she doing out there? She doesn't know how to surf." Sean's voice was filled with concern.

"I think she's been practicing all month," Elizabeth explained. Laurie was waiting for the perfect wave.

"Just like someone else I know." Sean sighed. "I really wanted you to win, Liz."

"I know, and I'm sorry. I hope those guys don't make you stick to the bet and work all those weekends," Elizabeth said.

"I don't care about that," Sean said. "I just think you deserved to win. I've never seen anyone pick up surfing the way you did. It was incredible."

Elizabeth shrugged. "I had a great time," she said. "And I *know* my friends were impressed— even if I did wipe out."

"Do you think you'll keep surfing?" Sean asked. "You should."

"I don't know. But if I do, I'll come back for some brush-up lessons, OK?"

"They'll always be on the house for you, Liz." Sean grinned at her. "And maybe next time we'll win something."

Elizabeth looked out at the ocean and saw Laurie catch a beautiful wave. "Look, Sean— Laurie's got her wave!"

Sean turned away from Elizabeth and stared at Laurie as she turned and began to slide along the wave. Her ride was going perfectly. She stayed up for what seemed like minutes. "Wow!" Sean gasped. "She's really good!"

Laurie doubled back and turned around and was obviously racking up points from the judges. Finally, when the wave began to crest, she pulled out of it beautifully. The whole crowd erupted into enthusiastic applause.

"I'll see you later, Liz. I want to congratulate Laurie!" Sean announced. When Laurie came out of the water, Sean ran up to her and swept her off her feet in a giant hug.

Mission accomplished, Elizabeth thought as she watched Laurie's face light up with a huge smile. The crowd was still cheering for Laurie's ride, and just for a second Elizabeth imagined how impressed all of her friends would have been if she had done as well as Laurie.

But I guess I didn't learn to surf just to prove to my friends I could be adventurous, Elizabeth thought. *I did it to prove something to myself.*

And now that she *had* proved to herself that she could be as daring as Jessica—or anyone else—Elizabeth had to admit she was looking forward to getting back to her old life, even if it was as predictable as everyone said.

And more than anything, she was looking forward to getting back to Todd.

"You were great!" Jessica cried. "But I still can't believe it was *you*!"

"You *better* believe it," Elizabeth answered, smiling.

"Does this mean we don't have to go to any marine biology presentation this afternoon? Or did you practice your surfing in spare moments away from the seaweed and turtle eggs?" Jessica asked.

"Don't worry, Jess," Elizabeth replied, her eyes shining with happiness. "There never *was* any marine biology project."

"Your wipeout was the most hysterical thing I've ever seen!" Jessica howled. "Your legs were flying up in the air, and you did a few flips and—I have to say it, Liz—you looked like a *total* klutz!"

"Some sister you are," Elizabeth said teasingly, wrapping a towel around her waist.

"Hey, Liz! Liz!"

Todd and Enid came running up to Elizabeth, and they both gave her big hugs.

"You were terrific!" Enid exclaimed. "Everyone had a hard time believing it was *you* at first!"

"Yeah," Todd said, "I thought I'd heard the name wrong."

"Well, what do you think of my big surprise?" Elizabeth asked Todd shyly.

"What do I think?" Todd answered, taking Elizabeth's hand and giving it a squeeze. "I think it was the funniest wipeout I've ever seen. But I know you had to have a lot of guts to get up there in the first place."

At that moment, the whole Sweet Valley group came rushing up to shake Elizabeth's hand and congratulate her. If Elizabeth didn't know better, she would have thought she had just won the first prize. And, in fact, she felt as if she had.

Elizabeth was walking toward the parking lot with Todd when Bill Chase came up beside her. Bill was a Sweet Valley student who had won a number of surfing competitons.

"Hey, Liz," Bill said, "can I talk to you a second?"

"Sure, Bill," Elizabeth said, stopping for a moment while Todd walked on ahead.

"Why did you decide to wipe out like that?" Bill asked, his expression incredulous. "It was the strangest thing I've ever seen!"

"You could *tell* that I wiped out intentionally?" Elizabeth asked, amazed.

"Of course I could tell," Bill exclaimed. "And I could also tell that you're a really good surfer, just by the way you got up on the board. I mean, you did *that* like a total pro. If you had just finished your ride, you might have gotten first place."

"Well, Bill," Elizabeth said, shrugging, "thanks for saying that. I did work really hard in the past month. But I had to mess up today . . . well, let's just say it was all in the name of romance."

"OK, Liz," Bill said, smiling and shaking his head. "Whatever you say."

Elizabeth glanced back toward the beach and was not surprised to see Sean and Laurie wrapped up in deep conversation, oblivious to everything else. It looked like her plan had worked. So what if everyone thought she was a klutz?

Elizabeth gave a satisfied sigh and ran to catch up with Todd.

"So tell me, surfer girl," Todd said as they left Moon Beach, "where can I take you to celebrate your surfing debut?"

"I've got an idea," Elizabeth said. "How about dinner at Mario's? But I need to go home and change first."

"Are you sure you don't want to go to the ocean somewhere, so you can study the surf?" Todd teased.

"Oh, I think I've had enough ocean to last for a while!" Elizabeth told him honestly. "I hope you're not mad that I kept the whole thing a secret from you," Elizabeth went on. "But I wanted to surprise everyone with how daring I could be."

"Oh, you *did*!" Todd laughed. "Believe me, you did!"

"And I really do feel great, just having taken a big risk," Elizabeth reflected. "Even if I didn't do too well."

"I guess it might have been fun to have a surfer-champion girlfriend," Todd remarked a few minutes later as he drove up to the Wakefield's house and parked his car. "But I'm much happier to have you back again, full-time."

"And I'm happy to be back!" Elizabeth exclaimed.

"Can I tell you something?" Todd asked shyly.

"Of course you can," whispered Elizabeth.

"I was awfully happy to find out that my only competition was a surfboard," Todd said, "and a borrowed one at that!"

"Oh, don't worry, Todd," Elizabeth whispered. "You don't have *any* competition at all." And she leaned over to give Todd a long and passionate kiss.

On Sunday afternoon Elizabeth and her brother, Steven, were wandering through the Sweet Valley Mall, keeping each other company as they ran errands. Steven was in his first year at the nearby State University. He had come home this weekend to start a month-long independent study project. While he did his research, he planned on seeing a lot of his girlfriend, Cara Walker, who was in the twins' class at Sweet Valley High.

"I need to visit the Sports Shop," Steven said, hurrying through the mall. "I mean, before you drag me into one of those clothing stores."

"Why do you want to visit the Sports Shop so badly?" Elizabeth asked, barely able to keep up with her brother's long strides.

"You're actually to blame for it," Steven responded.

"What do you mean?" Elizabeth asked.

"Well, you remember all those outdoor adventure magazines you bought a while ago, when you decided to be more adventurous?" he began. "The ones about surfing and scuba diving and hang gliding and everything?"

Elizabeth nodded.

"Well, I started reading one," Steven continued excitedly, "and I've decided to take up hang gliding."

"Hang gliding?" Elizabeth asked. "That can

be really dangerous, Steve—and expensive, too."

"Don't start worrying yet," Steven said as they walked into the Sports Shop. "I'm only here to find out more about lessons. Besides, you're the one who told the whole family how good it was for you to take some risks. I don't know how you did it, Liz, but you even convinced Mom and Dad that it had been a good idea."

"But that was only because I needed to prove something to *myself*," Elizabeth answered. "And you don't have the reputation of being conservative and predictable."

But when Steven decided on something, there was no changing his mind. They stayed in the Sports Shop long enough for him to ask a few questions about lessons, and then it was Elizabeth's turn to lead Steven into the Unique Boutique. After all the stories she had heard, Elizabeth was curious about the store.

"Oh, no," Steven moaned. "You're going to be in here all day trying things on."

"No, I'm not, I promise," Elizabeth answered. "I just want to look around."

As a salesgirl approached them, both Steven and Elizabeth were shocked into silence. The girl looked exactly like Steven's old girlfriend, who had died of leukemia months ago.

Steven turned as pale as a ghost. "Tricia?" he whispered at last.

"No, my name's not Tricia," the girl responded politely. "It's Andrea. Can I help you?"

Elizabeth could tell by the look on Steven's face that they needed to get out of the Unique Boutique as fast as possible.

"We're actually in a big hurry to get home, but thanks anyway," Elizabeth mumbled, dragging Steven back out into the mall.

As the two of them walked toward the car in stunned silence, Elizabeth thought, *So this is what Caroline was talking about that day at lunch.*

"I'm really sorry, Cara," Steven said later that afternoon, "but something just came up, and I don't think I can make it to the movies tomorrow. I have to get started on my Legal Ethics research."

"Oh, that's too bad," Cara said sadly. "I was really looking forward to seeing you."

"Don't worry, Cara," Steven said, "we'll get together soon."

"I *hope* so," Cara answered. "Because I don't see you enough as it is."

"I know," Steven replied. "I'll call you tomorrow."

As soon as Steven hung up the phone with Cara, he quickly dialed another number.

"Good afternoon, Unique Boutique. May I help you?" a woman asked.

"Is this Andrea?" Steven asked.

"Yes," she replied.

"You don't know me, but I was in your store today. My name is Steven Wakefield, and I was wondering if you'd consider going out with me tomorrow night."

What's going to happen between Cara and Steven now that Andrea's around? Find out in Sweet Valley High #64, THE GHOST OF TRICIA MARTIN.